Planet Reaping

Eric Kercher

Paper and Sword, LLC

For Oliver, an explorer of worlds.

From the Author

There are days when we all need an escape from a terrible job, a terrible day, or a terrible life.

Join my newsletter and get an escape from the real world, stories, and lore designed to entertain and delight.

You'll also get *Stories from the Deep*, an exclusive, unpublished anthology chock full of extra epilogues, short stories, and lore from the Patmos Sea Fantasy Adventure Series.

Join now at erickercher.com.

Enjoy the book.

-Eric Kercher

Prologue

THE BEHEMOTH AWAKES

They sent us to be their ambassadors and spies, the miners of life. We wanted domination, and we had the technology. The only part missing was the information we set about to find. So they loaded us up with supplies, patted us on the back, and sent us on our merry little way to traipse about the universe. They never told us we were never supposed to come back.

Bright steel glistened with starlight the first time he saw her from the window of the shuttle. The rays hit the metal and shattered into a million rainbow pieces against the great bulwark of the Prototype 15. She had passed the tests the others hadn't and was sitting in dock, ready for her commission. The yards were situated on a small hollowed out asteroid, but the 15 alone dwarfed the entire operation. Two other hulls, Hull 1 and 2, formed skeletons of advanced materials jutting out next to her. But 15, she was his boat. He could only look in awe at the curved sensuous body. It looked as if an egg had been cracked and pulled apart slightly, two cones connected by a tapered section that joined to the command center sphere in the middle. She looked nothing like the science fiction space ships of the past; new rules applied in space that the ancients had never thought of. As the shuttle grew closer she disappeared from view and the inner workings of the construction dock came into focus. He caught one last glimpse of her as the shuttle slid into dock.

He pulls a small object out of his pocket before he gets up to leave with the rest of the passengers. He opens the small trinket around in his hand and looks down to stare longingly at the picture and read the inscription one more time:

To my dearest Stephen, with all my love.

"Sir, we're disembarking, may I help you with anything?" a steward asks, shaking him from a motionless reverie.

"What - oh, no thank you." He snaps the locket shut and put it back into his front pocket. He takes a deep breath, gets up, and walks out of the cabin into the light.

Breaking Free

"Captain, we have a containment breach on the starboard engine hull." It had been nearly two minutes since the alarm bells had gone off and the Captain had taken his chair in his pjs, a white undershirt and boxers. The crew was lucky to have that.

"Mr. Long, where are we at?" Captain Tung swiveled over to look at his most junior officer and leader of the damage control team.

"Sir, we have the primary team away and are preparing the main team for breach." He looks unkempt and stressed, paper everywhere as he attempts his calculations. "They will be up in four - er, scratch that – five minutes."

"Very good." The captain turns back to his main console, watching the scene unfold. The logistics display did not look good. Second Mate Sellco sat in front of him, receiving reports as they came in and updating them.

"Sir, we have lost atmospheric pressure on the second deck of the starboard side. We will have massive casualties in thirty seconds and the ship will be inhospitable in two minutes."

"Stop the clock." The captain commanded, rising from his chair. Sirens cut off and flashing red lights turned a friendly shade of blue.

He picked up the microphone to the ship wide announcer. "This is the Captain speaking. Ladies and Gentlemen, let me remind you that we are on a mission of critical importance here. This level of competency will not cut it when we get out there, everyone needs to focus and remember their training. Return to your posts." He put the microphone back down. "Number two, consult." The executive officer finished showing the junior officer where his mistakes were and walked back to the captain.

"Sir, we need more time." The XO said. "I recommend we scale down the drill complexity." The captain pondered his words for a moment.

"I can see your point, but we can't go easier. I know this crew can handle your training regimen, this is about the whole ship coming together." He leaned in closer to his second in command. "The schedule has been moved up." He said, grim faced, "we no longer have the time we once did, they've ordered us out three months early."

"Three months!" the xo exclaimed softly "We can't have a crew ready by then!"

"I'm trying the best I can, but I at most can only buy us an extra month. We need to be ready XO." This time it was the xo's turn to ponder. "Give the crew an hour and run another set of drills."

"I'll draft up another training program. Like you said captain, we're going to need to be ready." The captain clapped the xo on the shoulder and dismissed him. He sat back down in his chair and reached up, feeling the small locket hung around his neck.

"Wait for me." He whispered. He stared out the window at the great expanse of space and felt alone.

The First Planet

They descended onto the first planet in the dead of the night in a remote location. The shuttle, completely dark to avoid notice, landed on a barren plain dotted with small boulders and shrubs. The bay doors opened and the infiltration crew had their first real look at the target planet. They had conducted a careful survey for weeks of the surface and had modified clothing to fit the local populous. Long, flowing robes of a material close to wool but harvested from the insides of underwater reeds covered the thick scaly mail breastplate and leggings of the men taken from local amphibian skin. At the men's side hung a thick metal club connected to their heavy wooden belt by a leather thong. But underneath it all was their technology. Recording devices manufactured into the fabric and skin captured a 360° view of their surroundings that fed to their ocular implants. As a result, they were able to have full perception of everything around them, something that only years of training could accustom them to. Sensor picked up even the most trace amounts of toxic chemicals and analyzed all substances to determine their atomic composition. Receivers transmitted all this information back to the ship and for data analysis. But the most important technology was the scanners.

These small devices took an image of the subject in question and completely mapped out bodily functions, including brain waves, which were sent back to the ship via the uplink. From there the information was processed and, if enough information was known, both emotions and mental processes could be mapped and predicted. This information was sent back to the ground team and brought t up in their mental displays. As a result they were able to predict the actions and almost read the thoughts of their target. With this equipment they were able to gather all the needed knowledge and store it for processing and analysis back on the research planet of Celiak.

Their purpose was pure, and they set about it with a desire and intensity that rivaled only the greatest conquerors and mathematicians in their quest for the truth. They began by assimilating into the planetary system, adopting personas and personalities unique to each member. Therese personalities were different than their own, but held the base of what they were. They established contact with each other rarely and sporadically to avoid detection, but they were always connected to the main ship. They uploaded regular reports and mined as much knowledge as they could for the computer to crunch.

They became teachers, constructions workers, doctors, sand scientists. Anything that would allow them to interact with a large number of people or a specifically high level of society. The day they stepped off the shuttle and stepped foot on the target planet they old self died and a new person was born for the deception to be complete. The crew was four, no more and no less, and they accepted the risks of a normal live that was not their own. Sometimes they married, had families and friends. All were abandoned after the period of learning. For because they were here, they knew their enemies as what they were. This is the story of their lives as officers of the Common Empire.

Dan Reich

He pulled his handkerchief out of his pocket and wiped the city grime off his glasses. At first he had marveled at how similar the green inhabitants were to him. In time, though, he had come to realize just how different they were. He spat a glob of tobacco into the gutter. It was a wonder they had taken that, the damn greenies. They were the descendants of a long line of environmentalists that had not taken too kindly to the industrialization of space and decided to populate their own planet free from the carbon emissions and noxious gasses created by "civilized" life. So they had all boarded a ship with their long greasy hair and cannabis and set out for the gem in the stars. They had landed on a barely inhabitable planet and called it Green. What they had landed on was so desolate it was no wonder that over 90% had died out in the first three months when their food generators had run out and no one in the colony had enough technical knowledge to do anything about it. But life goes on, and the remaining colonists had survived off the land, adapting and growing into a hardy species in the process.

The dust chocked up his throat and nose as he moved through the worksite, checking on various projects throughout the area. The survivors of the first great summer, as they called them, had lost some of their idealism and had resorted to using technology to achieve their ends, but they still choose to live a life of unburdenment to the environment. They had pulled down the dusty terraformers and created a large enough plot of farmland to last through the winter and sat down to have a powwow of sorts. They had debated and argued, and had headed fistfights in some cases, but they decided to move toward their original goal of complete sustainability on this new planet. For those who did not want to stay they arranged flights out on the second colony ship that arrived in time for the fresh mourning period of those who had died. In the end they decided that all future generations would have a choice and those not willing to live the lifestyle were to be given a seat on flights returning every year with new converts for the colony. Those were the first good years, but all good things must come to an end.

He surveyed the new colonist building, a completely sustainable building being constructed for the ever growing ministry of green preservation. Sun collectors taken from and made of small deposits of metal found in the desert mines produced energy and sent it to the collection gird. The earthen walls bore no taint of harvested material, but were packed between trees that had been grown for generations specifically for this purpose. The intertwined branches carefully molded throughout the trees lifetime grew into a beautiful patchwork roof in the summer, and were covered in the winter with grasses to support the snowfall and keep the building dry and warm. Water was piped through hollow grass tubes, much like the bamboo of his planet but far more flexible. The installers were putting in this in now, trying to weave it through the branches.

"No, no, that's not the right conduit." Dan said. "Notice how the branches go over in this area, that's the support loading beam, you want this u beam right here." He pointed to a slightly lower branch and the technician weaved it through and grinned sheepishly. Dan nodded and moved on. It had been hundreds of generations after the original colonists had arrived to this point in time. A few generations after the landing the new colonists just stopped coming. There was a time when it was extremely popular but people soon realized the reality of the situation and either left, died, or conformed. It did help though, when a young woman decided to take matters into her hands. Petty squabbling had been going on for years, but it was slowly escalating. As soon as the new ships stopped coming those who disagreed with the lifestyle found nowhere to go. Some converted, but most didn't. They moved and found each other, rejecting the majority. Soon, they were growing stronger as they were unhindered in their technology to build and create. They began creating weapons and real battles began to break out. Raids, a t first, but they soon quickly escalated into skirmishes, and then full battle. And then a savior appeared. She united the various tribes that had developed using her feminine charm; she had men eating out of her hand within moments of meeting her. At first, she tried to use her power to convert, but the ones who had rejected the colony were beyond saving. They surprised the unbelievers in the night, the unbelievers fought wither their technology and weapons but sheer numbers and surprise were against them. The colonists ransacked their towns and slaughtered everyone. But she knew it would not last, as long as their belief remained strong there would be doubters. So she established a strong government on the principles of their community, and set workers to monitor the masses for any rule breaking. Now, Mother Nature would truly be protected, for she had a valiant defender. The ministry of green preservation was created and given the most advanced forms of technology available to keep everything orderly and in compliance. But the first matriarch, Janine, knew that she would eventually perish and set a strong system in place to elevate only the most fanatical to the highest levels of office. She dissolved the power she had into a council, a puppet council, which followed the will only of the leader. From that point on, the power she had was secure.

He walked to the wall crew who were packing the final layer of clay onto the timber substructure of the wall. he inspected them as they worked, scooping up mounded piles of dry earth, adding water and packing tightly against the old layer using wooden pilings. Since the clay was not particularly prone to sticking the walls ended up being steeply sloped. They had been doing a good job, and their clay seemed better than most batches that came in now a days. He pulled out a wooden protractor and measured the angle. 23°. He whistled.

"Great work boys. This is the best angle I've seen in years." The crew smiled at each other and got back to work, more gung ho than they had been. Dan smiled inwardly and then continued his rounds. That was the best angle he had seen in years, by five degrees. Inwardly something did not feel right, but he kept moving. He checked the sun and realized he didn't have much time left, curfew was coming in an hour and he had some more work to get done with on the plans for the perimeter before nightfall. He went to check out the final crew, the tree gardeners pulling down the orientation stakes that helped the branches grow in the right direction and headed over to his temporary office. The workers were packing up and all trickling out now, he only had a half hour before curfew. He sighed. These days the jobs were tougher and the hours longer. He tromped over to the temporary shelter and looked at the plans on the table, wooden, of course, the only material allowed for most things. He poured over the charts and drawings, checking the timetable. They were nearly a week ahead. In all his years, he had never been ahead on a job. Ever. Something nagged at him, what was going on? Something was wrong here. He went back to the worksite, a hunch stirring within him. He went up to the freshly constructed wall and pulled a vial from a secret compartment in his belt. He scraped a sample off the wall and put it back in the compartment. Using his implants he contacted mother ship and requested analysis of the clay. Within seconds he had a readout. Silica, clay, and something else: bauxite. He had solved his mystery; someone had been adding chemicals to the composition to help it stick better. That was against regulations and had some very bad consequences associated with it. He scratched his head. Who would even want to do this? He went back outside to a large bin where the clay was kept. There were only four people who needed access to this, himself and the three wall workers. The question is which one it was. He took a sample of the remaining clay and processed it. This stuff was clean. He glanced up at the sky. Just as he looked up the curfew bell sounded. Fifteen minutes. He pulled out a small recording device from his sleeve, designed to look like a wooden button, and placed it in the mixing bucket next to the bin where the workers added the water to get the clay. He set up contact with eh mother ship for constant surveillance throughout the next 24 hours. Whoever made the mix for tomorrow would be seen. But now, it was time to go home. He quickly walked back to his foreman's shed, grabbed his lunch pail and headed home.

That night he got home, kissed his wife hello and bedded down just in time for bedtime. Throughout the city there was a mandatory lights out period, as lights causes both light pollution and uses energy. Therefore, no lights were allowed except in the very special case, such as government work, where it was absolutely essential to be up past sunset. Dan, like most people, occasionally went out to watch the stars, but mainly just went to bed with the sun. As he dozed off, he had the images of all three wall workers in his mind buzzing about. Which one could it be? With it playing in his mind he drifted off to sleep.

The next morning he woke with a start. The sky was still dark, but the hints of a sun were just beginning to peak up beyond the horizon. He got up, warmed some coffee to the regulated temperature and sat in a chair to watch a glorious sunrise. Soon the whole household was up and he grabbed his packed lunch, kissed his wife goodbye, and set off for work, the thoughts of the perpetrator spinning in his mind. He walked the short route to the new building and noticed a small commotion. A few of the workers and unfamiliar people were already there, milling about. He checked the sky and realized that he had been a few minutes late. "That's odd" he thought to himself. And then he noticed the white sheet draped over a suspiciously human shaped object next to the half-finished building. He walked up to the group.

"Are you the foreman?" one of the unfamiliar faces asked.

"I am" he replied. Clearly this man was a lawman, much like the policemen of his society sworn to enforce the laws of the colony. He was taller than most, with a stern face and unsmiling eyes, crow's feet lacing the corners. This lawman had been in his job quite a while.

"I'd like to ask you a few questions" the lawman pulled out a notebook and pencil.

"What's going on?" Dan asked.

"Sir, there's been a murder. Last night, one of the plumbers called it in earlier this morning. They said you were usually the last one to leave at night."

"That's right, who was it?"

"From what we know right now it was Jacob Hanassy, a member of your wall crew." Ice gripped Dan's heart, and memories of the unauthorized content flashed unbidden to his thoughts. He pulled out a handkerchief and blew his nose into it.

"That's horrible" he said after a moment. He had known Jake fairly well, one of the more competent members of his whole crew. Pieces started falling into place; he was intelligent enough to start messing with the wall composition. "Please, let me know what I can do to help."

"Do you know of anyone that may have a reason to kill Mr. Hanassy?"

"No, he was a pretty likeable guy. Kind of quiet sometimes, well, most of the time. He did his job well and was friends with the other crewmates though." The lawman began scribbling in his notebook, writing down what Dan was saying. "As far as I know he was doing well in life too, he had a wife and a kid on the way. "

"Well you can tell me what you were doing last night from when you were seen to this morning."

"Well I was the last person to leave last night, like you mentioned I usually am. We had had some troubles with a few of the designs so I was looking over the plans again. I lost track of time and had to rush home after I heard the curfew bells- this is terrible, Jake was one of the most intelligent men on the crew." Dan said

"And after?" the lawman asked, looking up from his notebook and pausing his scribbling

"I went to bed and woke up this morning."

"Do you have someone how can confirm that?" the lawman asked

"Yes- my wife. Am I a suspect?" Dan stared at the lawman, slightly confused by understanding. The lawman met his gaze with steely eyes.

"Everyone is a suspect at this point Mr. Reich." He said, breaking eye contact and putting away his notebook. "We still have to check the deceased's place of residency and contact the family but we will let you know if we need anything else. For now we have to cordon off the area until the mortician can arrive. Go home Mr. Reich, we'll be in touch." More crewmembers were arriving and the few lawmen were questioning all of them. Dan turned and told everyone they were free for the day due to the accident, as soon as they had checked with the lawmen. Those men who had arrived before him began to leave.

Thoughts began to flow in Dan's head. Somehow, there was something bigger in this. Jake really did have no enemies, his network told him that. For all intents and purposes he was completely clean. This had to do with the wall composition somehow, and he suspected Jake was doing the alterations. His smile had seemed a bit bright when he complemented the crew yesterday, and he certainly knew enough about the mix to get him in trouble. He was itching to recover his recorder, but with the lawmen swarming the place he had to be discreet.

He began to take inventory, making sure all the materials were still there. He began in the shed, checking on the blueprints and administrative documents. Sure enough, nothing had been touched let alone stolen. He went out into the yard and checked on all the building materials too. Each post had everything in hand. As he made his way to the mixing station he asked for a quick personnel scan from the mother ship. Thankfully, all the lawman were preoccupied with questioning the crewmembers and he was able to discreetly collect his recorder and put it back into his uniform mainframe. He dumped the information to the mother ship and asked for them to analyze it for any persons and to see what they could find out about it.

He left then, returning back the way he had come for six months now. Along the way he stopped at a small hill overlooking the city. A conglomerate of trees and plants planned into a city, it was beautiful. The canopy roofs twisted in the breeze and it seemed to be a paradise. But he knew that these people had bent the plants to their will and he had a suspicious feeling someone had bent these people to theirs.

Stan Super

The process had always been kicking and screaming. He pulled out the baby and wrapped the squalling thing in sanitized cloth. No matter what it was, ideas or a person, the real thing always was born kicking and screaming. He handed the small thing to its mother after wiping off the blood and grime of the birth. She was exhausted but smiling. It always amazed him that they always did that, that all that pain led to something good. He gave his congratulations to the mother and made his way out to the father, directing the nurses to clean things up and take care of the mother. He pulled off his gloves and washed them, prepping them for the sanitization cycle. He did the same for his surgical clothes, dyed blood red to hide the real thing. He threw the prepared clothing into the sanitizer and started it. Then he washed his face, threw on his doctor coat and walked out to meet the father.

The father, Fred Morrgan, was pacing nervously up and down the corridor leading to the waiting room. He was clearly agitated and the moment he saw Dr. Super he nearly ran up to him.

"What's the news Doc? Are thy ok?" Fred pleaded, looking for a hint of news in the doctor's eyes.

"Relax Fred, you have a beautiful baby girl and Margery is going to be fine." The nervousness washed from the face of Fred and happiness took its place. He clasped the doctor's hand, grinning from ear to ear, knees visibly shaking.

"I'm a father!" Fred exclaimed. Stan felt himself smiling, caught up by the happiness of the moment. These were the most rewarding moments of his job, when the sickness and pain were all gone and something new and whole and healed was standing in its place. It almost made him forget his mission. Almost. Smiling, the doctor led Fred back to the now clean mother and daughter in the hospital room. He left them there and began his rounds.

Drugs were hard to come by on this colony. Since its inception it had taken on the responsibility of never releasing any dangerous chemicals and toxic materials into the environment. Unfortunately, highly effective and powerful medicines required process that gave off these sort substances. As a result, since the war of preservation most medicines that had been developed had been outlawed. Now all the medicine was either herbal or natural. For some things that was fine, but it was almost a miracle for a successful treatment of some diseases that had been all but eradicated on the Homeworld. He shook his head as he looked at the chart of his first patient. He had undergone a routine appendectomy and had developed a staph infection. The few antibiotics they had developed were soon rendered useless by the adaptive strains of bacteria and had been an almost unsolvable problem. Huge waves of death had forced the ministry of green preservation to ease some rules into medical applications, but only to trim the deaths down to a manageable level. Manageable by their studies ended up being thousands of dead a year, but was a far cry from the millions of casualties before the easing.

He finished his rounds and returned to his office, pushing the thoughts to the back of his mind. As primitive as the technology was they still had developed advanced methods of dealing with pain using the land. Instead of pharmacologists, herbologists had ruled the day. Whether it was rubbed on, ingested, inhaled, or injected the herbs of this planet had proved somewhat useful. More importantly was the ability of the colonists to reorganize pain within their own body. They had developed advanced breathing and muscle control techniques that relegated pain to the mind where it could be processed and stored as information and not as a crippling illness. As a result, recovery times were somewhat faster and less pain medication was needed. That is, if they did end up recovering.

Stan sat down at this desk and began to pour over paperwork. It surprised him how much it was a part of the colony government. All of it was recycled, now dyed a gray tinge from the corruption of inks, abut there was still an inordinate amount of it. He scanned and uploaded all of this to the mother ship and had begun tracking trends and patterns in the illnesses. Certain individuals were found infected with a rare disease that currently had neither a treatment nor a cause. This had been going on for quite some time now, and it only affected a small number of the population, but the first sings of it had come some years after the war of preservation. He took off his glasses and rubbed his eyes as he uploaded the new forms to the mothership. He was tired after the sixteen hour birth, hospitals were some of the few building swallowed lights for night occupation and work, and he needed to sleep. But this problem was bugging him. He picked up the chart of the latest victim, one Tim York, and got back up. One patient, then he would go home for some rest.

As he walked into Tim's room he could see that the man did not have long to live. The disease affected the breathing system the hardest, and from the rasping he heard Tim's lungs had already progressed beyond the point of recovery. Soon he would develop an inflammation in the esophagus and it would constrict until he would not be able to breathe. For now, he had at least a few days and was still strong enough to converse.

"Good afternoon Tim." The man had not seen the Doctor enter, his eyes gazing off into the world just outside his window. He turned now and noticed him for the first time.

"Good afternoon doctor." Tim was a younger man, in his prime, before the illness had struck. He had come in with a small cough that would not go away. He had been strong and fit then, but the weeks of bed rest had softened his muscles and now the skin hung off his almost emaciated figure. He had only been able to eat through a straw lately; his whole foods would only come back up if he could manage to get them down.

"How are you Tim?"

"I've certainly been better." The exhausted man attempted a small laugh, but it only ended in a coughing fit. The Doctor smiled politely, cringing inside at the response. Not much time left at all.

"We still are working on something, I did get your test results back yesterday from the blood test and you do have high levels of oxygen still in your blood stream." The doctor latched onto the only good news he had, even though they both knew it was futile to think he could recover. "Thanks doc, but everyone knows no one recovers from the Choking death." The doctor reached out his hand and patted Tim on the shoulder.

"You fight this Tim; don't give up whatever you do." Stan had sent samples of the first patient he encountered with the disease back to the mother ship. The doctors there had determined the cause of the disease within days and had developed a cure within weeks. Small particles had entered Tim's body, nanobots, and were now wreaking havoc on his insides. They would break down his cells and uses the resultant building blocks to fabricated clones. Once a certain concentration was reached in the blood stream then the bots began to attack the respiratory system, breaking down the diaphragm, lungs, and esophagus. Most people died before their lungs were gone, from the inflammation of the esophagus, but the ones who lasted past that with the help of tubing soon were unable to work their diaphragm, and then they would die. Costly and rare Breathing machines worked for a few days after the diaphragm had disintegrated, but the lungs were two steps behind.

"Thanks Doc." He smiled a genuine smile then, grateful for the support. Stan pulled up a chair that was sitting in the corner to his bedside.

"May I ask you some questions about your personal life Tim?" there had to be some other force at work here, and Stan intended to find out what.

"Sure, go ahead."

"These may be odd to you, but I'm trying to find something out that may lead to something." The hardest part of knowing there was a cure was not administering it. But Stan knew that if the mother ship was able to send down a supply undetected and if they were able to get it to him, the world he now inhabited would be thrown into compromise should he administer it. They were observers here, and that would compromise the situation. "Did you do anything new before you developed the cough, were there any changes in your life? Be completely honest with me." These people may be enemies as far as the mission was concerned, but it still hurt him to use them, knowing their humanity firsthand.

"Well, as you know, I am a researcher for the aquatics and bionautics institute arm of the ministry of green preservation. The only thing I can think of was our new project we had begun work on." Tim paused then, recalling memories of better times. The doctor sat in silence, waiting for his answer. "We were determining the effects of recycling pollution on river tributaries from the paper plants, to see if the new machines put into development had upset anything. I had just started running tests outside the new river when I got sick."

"Was anyone else working with you?" the doctor questioned, a suspicion flag rising in his mind.

"No, we don't have enough force to have teams do this, usually its one person per problem."

"So what's happening to the project now?"

"It will likely be disbanded, these project s take months to complete and the department had its arms full lately, with the pushes to reform. Bureaucracy tends to do things like that, and we were up to our knees in it." Tim was a good man, and held to his beliefs steadfastly. He was also extremely stubborn, refusing some treatments because they put too much toxic waste into the environment. It was obvious someone wanted this project to die and Tim was not likely to give it up for any reason. He was also notorious for raising a fuss when projects proved the environment was harmed. The ministry always backed him.

"I'm sorry to hear that." The doctor's mind was moving furiously now. A soft knock came at the door. He turned around to see Belinda, Tim's wife, standing at the doorway.

"Am I interrupting anything?" Belinda asked hesitantly.

"No, not at all!" Stan exclaimed, "Please, come in, come in." he stood and ushered her in and she cautiously entered. She was a shy girl, and worked herself to the bone since Tim had gotten sick. She was only able to see him a small amount each day because of the curfew. "I will leave you two alone- Tim, I can talk to you later." He stifled a small objection as Tim raised his hand and opened his mouth. "Good night you two." With that, the doctor departed.

He felt no exhaustion know, exhilarated by the breakthrough. Someone clearly wanted Tim dead, and they had done it. The choking death was like a surgeon's knife, killing only those targeted and never spreading to anyone else. It was like the disease was specifically tailored to one person, and it may be knowing what the mother ship had discovered. There was something behind all of this, and he had a sneaking suspicion he knew who. He returned to his office and locked the door. He made contact with the mothership, this time risking a transmission to report his findings.

"This is Agent Yellow, I have recently mad a breakthrough on the research of the choking death disease. My latest victim was working on a project to determine the pollution content of the new river when he was infected. As a result of his death, the project will be discontinued and lost in the bureaucracy. I would request an investigation into the content of the New river and possibly the ministry itself. End transmission." He packaged the report and sent it to the mothership for deliberation. He waited for the confirmation they had received it, and once they had he sat back in his chair, gazing out the window at the sunset as the curfew bells began to ring. He smiled slightly, they were making progress.

Jan Young

She had always been a no nonsense kind of person, even at the academy. Here most rebellious act had been joining the service in the first place; to teach others the lessons they needed to stay in line. It was no accident that she had become the teacher in the group, affecting the minds even though she wasn't supposed to. And she was doing that right now as well. She peered up from her book, gazing around at the bright little faces furiously working on the assignment. She nodded approvingly and returned to her reading. Out of the corner of her eye she saw movement that was not the familiar scribbling of young children.

"John Appleby you get back to work before I have to have a conference." The little boy unfolded the piece of paper he had been turning into a device of destruction into her perfectly structured afternoon, a paper airplane, and picked up his pencil to continue writing, cheeks as red as her marks that would no doubt be on his page tomorrow. Everyone in the class knew what a "conference" was to Miss Young, and many behinds were sore because of them. No, her dominion was tidily nonsense free. She looked up once more from here reading, about the sociological struggle in the war of preservation just as the timer ran out of sand.

"Pencils down!" she commanded as she stood up. Harried children groaned as they put down their writing utensils, knowing the consequences of a bad grade. "Sheets to the front!" reluctantly they handed their papers forward to the next student before them. They then automatically passé d them to the right to form a neat pile on the head of the classes desk. Mary, the head of the class for today, smugly stood up, straightened the pile, then gracefully took the papers to hand them to Jan's outstretched hand.

"Here are the papers Miss Young." Mary said in a prim tone, glancing back to Sally, the usual competition for the head desk. Sally, her face dark with jealousy, slid deeper into her second desk chair. Jan smiled at Mary, to encourage the competition, and waved her away.

"Thank you child, you may return to the head desk." Jan neatly and deftly tucked the papers into her purse and pulled out her notes for the next section. Inwardly, she sighed. Another lesson on the importance of human effects on the environment. It didn't surprise her that there were so many lessons, but it did aggravate her that they all said the same thing. Well, better to be on with it then. The children had descended into a tumult of whispers and she rapped the desk to get their attention.

"Class you must remember the effect of your actions upon this world. The ministry of green preservation has recently caught a ring of five offenders that would pollute the world you live in. they were found burning unauthorized amounts of wood to stay warm in the northern hemisphere late last week. Tell me class, what consequences does burning wood bring to the environment?"

"Carbon dioxide emissions." The class monotone in unison

"Very good, and why are these emissions bad?" hands shot up across the classroom but Sally's was up first. "Sally." Sally stood up, glared at Mary, then snobbily answered.

"Because the releasing of these emissions, also known as greenhouse gasses, causes the sunlight to be trapped in the atmosphere, warming up the earth and causing great calamities." She had given the textbook response. Jan followed the outline on the mandatory ministry of green preservation publication.

"And what else causes carbon dioxide to be released?" Jan asked the class, this time noticing a little boy named Eric beat both the girls with his hand up. "Eric." He stood up.

"Humans breathing." He answered proudly, "but we plant a tree every Saturday and sleep a certain amount of time and not be allowed to do large amounts of exercise otherwise the ministry takes you away." Jan blinked at the last part of his answer.

"Takes you away? No, no- Eric, they don't take you away right away. What happens first is that they make you pay the world back, then the offenders who rightly fail to repent get one more chance. After that the ministry has to make them stop, for the good of the world." He was right about everything, and it chilled her slightly to think about it. But she didn't need to worry, she followed all the rules. Except, of course, for all her equipment. Better not to think of that though. "Does everyone understand that?" she asked the class.

"Yes, Miss Young." They replied together.

"Good, now Eric, take a point off your daily score for not present-ing the whole truth." Abashedly, he sat down and dejectedly hung his head. "But add three points for three methods of restitution we pay for our harm upon the planet." He perked up and added the points to his score. She would tally up the class and announce the new head of class based on the scores in the morning. "and now we will review the full five methods of restitution and they are-" she began scribbling on the board "Technology disuse, sleep control, tree planting, exercise discouragement, and environmental cleaning." pencils scratched on paper as they wrote down on their notes what she was listing.

"The first, technology disuse, is the most important. In the ages before the green colony humans polluted the world just to have a pot of coffee or see their friends down the road. Since the arrival and again in the war of preservation we have realized that technologies that make our lives easier also destroy the very planet we inhabit. As a result only certain technologies are allowed, and for only certain things. For example, the ability to use computers has been known for ages, but only the ministry of green preservation is allowed to use them as the ill effects on the environment are too great to support a full population using them."

"The next, sleep control, allows us to better control our carbon dioxide emission by slowing our breathing and producing less. That is why you are not required to wear your pollution detector at night, that and the sensors that are in your house monitor that as well." They were all wearing the pollution detectors, hats that sensed internal temperature, heartbeat, breath, and all functions of the body. Jan had discovered that the information was packaged and transmitted to the ministry of green preservation via transmissions. Thankfully, that is what allowed them to package data to transmit to the mother ship as well, disguised as such transmissions. The detector ran off the heat from the body, and needed and had no use for batteries.

"Tree planting is one of the most rewarding ways of showing penance. For in this way we create things that will be fostered by our very pollution, because trees need what to survive?" She paused and hands shot up into the air. "Mary." Mary stood up."

"Carbon dioxide Miss Young." Mary smugly replied.

"Excellent, add a point." Mary sat back down and struck another tally, shooting Sally a smug look. "And everyone knows that all humans must plant a tree a day until their 15th birthday. Then it is their responsibility to care for and nurture that grove for the rest of their life. In this way we balance ourselves with nature."

"Now exercise can be very rewarding, and we can use its effects to work even harder to protect the environment, but too much exercise causes a massive increase in respiration, and consequently, a large increase in carbon dioxide emission. That is why we only have physical education one day a week." She looked out over the class and realized this rule may not be the best, based on the relatively pudginess of the average class member. She herself had been gaining weight due to the restrictions; she wasn't able to run as much as she had during training.

"And the final restitution is environmental cleaning. Every month all are required to go out into nature and work to clean the environment. The ministry of green preservation picks the projects we all work on and together we will reverse the adverse effects of our society on the planet." At this point she had covered all the topics except one.

"And remember, should anyone violate the laws and cause pollution to the earth you must immediately tell me, even if you have the faintest glimmer of a suspicion. This includes your parents and siblings, because sometimes they don't even realize that they are doing it. Does everyone understand?" the class all nodded.

"Yes Miss Young." They responded.

"Good, now the end bell is about to ring, but before it does check your tallies." As soon as she finished the bell that signaled the end of the school day rang, and Jan felt a small measure of satisfaction. "Now, all of you run along home." They all began to quickly gather their bags and books, careful not to cause too much of a commotion. As soon as they reached the door they exploded into cheerful conversation and hurriedly ran to get away from the place. Jan tidied up her desk as they went, organizing the tests and class notes. Leaning down, she put them into her purse and stood up to the figure of Joseph standing in front of her desk. She peered at him from behind her glasses. He cleared his throat nervously and began to mumble.

"Miss Young...um...I...you said that we should, well..." he trailed off, looking down at his shoes.

"Say what you need to say child, I don't have time for this." Was her curt reply. He looked back up, cheeks flaming.

"I-I think I need to report my parents." He blurted out, looking relieved at the outburst. Jan sat back in her chair, shocked. This was the first time any student had ever reported to them about anyone. It had happened too many of her friends; usually the children went to the counselor first, because they were more popular and easy on them. A few moments passed as she realized the gravity of the situation. He did not know it but he had.

"Well, pull up a chair child and let me hear this." She stood up and walked over to the door, looking up and down the halls, noticing only a few stragglers, shut the door and locked it. By the time she returned to her desk Joseph had pulled a chair close to hers and was sitting. She sat down and pulled out a pad and pencil, all a show because she left her recorders on at all times during the school day to pick up everything she could. "Now, tell me what you think is wrong." She had taken a softer tone, enticing the story out of him without scaring him. She was surprised he had the courage to approach her, alone nonetheless, and there was valuable information to be gained here.

"Well, my mother and father keep talking about wrong things, things that they shouldn't be saying. They keep confusing me because they tell me all the things you do and everything we should know but I can hear them late at night from their room. I sometimes sneak to their door because I get lonely at night." Joseph paused, realizing he had just said something embarrassing. Jan moved a hand to his shoulder to comfort him.

"Don't worry; this is a secret for just you and me. No one else will know what you said." She gave him a rare smile, she knew how to control people and sometimes the stick wasn't always the best way. The young boy took a breath and prepared to go on.

"Well, they keep talking about how to leave, how it wasn't right that the ministry was controlling everything. They say that the rules are oppressive and lately they said that they needed to do something." He stopped, tears welling in his eyes. "They're going to ruin everything." He cried, "Can't they see that?" he burst into tears. Jan tried to comfort him, patting his shoulder.

"There, there, everything will be okay. I'm sure that they aren't trying to hurt you or anyone." She said reassuringly. He blubbered on for a few more moments, then began to settle down. He sniffled into his sleeve and wiped his eyes. They had become red with tear and he looked up at her finally, his eyes still glistening.

"I did the right thing, didn't I?" He asked, full of trepidation and anticipation.

"Yes you did child, yes you did." Her stomach churned at the lie. She had no ideas what would happen to his parents now, but it would soon be out of her hands. His eyes showed his relief and he visibly relaxed.

"Thank you Miss Young, may I go now?" she waved him away and he collected his things and left. She sat back in her chair, this had been a breakthrough but it felt horrible to her. They had not been here long, but she had already earned the trust of some of the children. And now they were spying on their parents. It was ironic, but she would take what she could get at this point. The implications of what had just happened now came to her mind. The reporting process was a lengthy one, and secret. The ministry had a large role in the process, and she would have access to some high level officials. Her ears began tingling, like they always did when she got excited. What a glorious day! She looked out the window to the bright sunlight streaming in. the children had all left by now, but the courtyard the classroom looked out on was still rife with life and growing things. That was the best part of this planet, the gardens. She stared for a bit longer than realized she needed to be home before the curfew. She grabbed her bag and headed out the door, pausing to look back on the tidy classroom before she shut the door. She had kept her forms at home just for such an occasion.

Jan walked out of the enormous one story building. It had been designed with windows, but the thin pieces of glass were murky because they were made without byproducts. Through the window the gardens had looked good, now they were gorgeous. She walked down the dirt path, careful to not step on the grass, to the road. It was made of a special type of grass that was grown specifically for road beds, which grew a deep red. Carts and one person vehicles that reminded her of bicycles on the home world whizzed by, but she kept to the sides of the road. Her mood was ruined when a bicycle like two seated foot powered wagon, called a carrier, flew by her a little too fast and rattled her hair. But she only lived a few minutes away so the trip was soon over.

Her residence was a smaller quaint house, made of only a few trees packed together with dirt. She lived alone so she had no need of a sprawling mansion, and, although they could afford it with their ability to replicate the green currency of small weights of stone, that would have given away far too much information and may have compromised the mission. She lovingly stroked her beautiful flower hedge, trimmed to perfection on the weekends, and briskly walked up her stone path. She checked the mail bin and collected her mail. Shuffling through it she opened the door. Her lips pursed when her eyes fell upon a slightly different looking envelope. She placed this odd package in her purse and filed the rest into two bins on a table just inside the door. One was labeled "Bills" and the other "Follow-up" in a flowery handwriting. Her house was completely spotless, everything in order, separated in two rooms. The door opened into the kitchen, the living room, and her personal library while a wall cordoned off the bedroom with an attached bathroom. It wasn't much, but it was normal for a teacher of her position. She pulled out a few vegetables and beans and began heating them on her electric stove. Meat was hard to come by, as animals also polluted the environment with their bodies, but things that grew out of the ground were in abundance. She checked the battery and sighed. The partly cloudy day hadn't filled up her battery bank and she would only get a lukewarm meal this evening. Such was the nature of her work.

While her meager meal was being prepared she got to work on the task she had been excited about. The first step was to fill out the necessary paperwork, which she pulled out from the small desk stashed in the corner by her library. It didn't take long and the curfew bells where just ringing by the time she had finished. It was all there, neatly in her report. The incident with Joseph, his story, and everything else the ministry of green preservation needed to confirm it. She placed that in her purse and got down to the real business. She left her recorders on all the time, and now she was uplinking to the mother ship to download the data to their mainframe. They were never supposed to develop a pattern, some days she did it in the morning, some at night, sometimes weeks went by without a transmission, and sometimes she needed to make more than a few a week. This time, she knew she had information extremely valuable to the mission so she wasted no time at all. She did a quick security sweep to reveal intruders or spies and established contact. She then uploaded everything to them, keeping a copy of the interview with Joseph for future reference. People always assume she had a perfect memory, and she wasn't about to tell them that she kept a copy of almost everything in her head, but with Joseph's she put a priority tag on for easy recovery.

As soon as mother ship had gotten everything she requested dismissal and was given it. She shut down the transmission quickly, she never liked taking risks at all. They had given her instruction to continue her investigation and she began forming plans. Whatever happened, she would soon be in contact with government officials, and most would be high ranking. She could not afford a misstep, she had to get in as deep as possible to learn as much as she could without revealing herself. She began to formulate a plan, and soon had what she thought was workable in her head. Then she began to plan contingency plans, just in case someone did something she hadn't anticipated. From all the reports though, she could use their bull headed beliefs to her advantage and come out with them none the wiser. That done, she pulled out the papers and began to tally scores.

She finished just before the last of the light began to vanish, sinking in the horizon like a stone in water and splashing beautiful colors across the sky. "Whatever people think of me I can still appreciate beauty", she told herself. Others had labeled her as cold, calculating, and emotionless. She was all but the latter. There was a difference between having emotions and controlling them, in her opinion. Her work finished, and Mary still at the head of the class, she fixed herself for bed and fell asleep with the sun.

The next morning she awoke fresh and excited. She got up and made breakfast, selecting one of her choice novels as reading material for the task. The title of it was "Wilderness Fire" and her friends would have been surprised to know she even had a copy, let alone she enjoyed it. But the writing was good, and the characters believable, so that was what drew her to it, is what she told herself. If she was honest she would admit the steamy romance scenes were the real draw, they were so believable. After breakfast she gathered her things and headed out the door to school. The sun was just peeking above the horizon.

Instead of walking straight to her classroom she instead took a detour to the administrator's offices. Form in hand, she walked straight past the secretary to the counselor's office. She strode in to catch the portly man in the midst of taking off his jacket. His eyes showed surprise, both at the unexpected interruption and the unexpected individual before him.

"Ah, Miss Young." He said, eyes darting to the open door and back to her. "Please, come in." he was well trained in the art of bureaucracy and there was only a small hint of sarcasm in his voice.

"Thank you Mr. Malone." She strode over to his desk and plunked the form into his inbox. "I believe this may be of interest to you." If he was surprised at her entrance, he was baffled by the actions she had taken. She waited while he took off his coat, and when he had turned around to look at her questioningly she replied in turn. "A standard suspicious persons report, I believe you will find everything filled out correctly and in order." He cleared his throat.

"Ah, yes-erm, well for this sort of thing we need to have a follow up interview." He had made his way to his desk and picked up the form. "I will notify the authorities and they will need you to be ready sometime tonight." He stared at the page, scanning it for mistakes.

"Very well, they know where to find me. Good day." With that she turned and left briskly. Her room was exactly how she left it, neat and orderly, and by the time she got there the sunlight was streaming in the windows, lighting the place up. Instead of using electric lighting the canopy ceiling held special rods of glass that pulled the light in from outside and lit up the inside. It was quite effective at channeling light, however, once the sun went down, so too your light. She pulled out the lessons of the day and prepared for her class.

They came to her after the school day was over and the children were gone. She had suspected that they would and she ticked off a tally in her head. So far, so good. They were somewhat unassuming, dressed normally but in black with the pollution monitors like everyone else. They knocked on her door as she was grading papers for the day.

"Miss Young, may we have a word?" there were two of them, one taller and skinnier and one shorter and more squat. Their eyes were harder than their bodies though, and she could tell these men were dangerous.

"Yes, yes, do come in." She beckoned them inside and rose, directing them to desks she set up for the purpose. They entered calmly and sat in the too small chairs meant for children.

"We're here about the report." One man pulled out a small notebook and pencil and began to take notes. What of, she had no idea, because they were the ones doing the talking. "First off, have you observed anything to cause you suspicion that Joseph is prone to…imaginative storytelling or doubt in the curriculum?" his eyes bored into hers.

"no, as far as I can tell Joseph has taken to the teachings very well." She needed to be careful now, Joseph's parents were not the only ones who had something on the line anymore. Her own teaching and beliefs would be called into question now, just as a "precaution." She continued. "I would say he may have the best grasp of the concepts put out by the ministry of green preservation. As for imagination, I'm afraid he may be a little bit short in that department." All of it was true, in reality he was not that smart. He had swallowed everything she had to teach hook, line, and sinker. The short man continued to write in his book. They would not give their names, they were supposed to be anonymous. That means they were far up indeed.

"Very good" the tall man continued "now please account the facts as you know them of the day you were approached by Joseph, including the lesson for the day." She paused for effect, bringing up the interview to her mind.

"Well, we had math in the morning, grammar, and then science...oh, and the statement put out by the ministry was last." She tapped her finger against her lips. "Essentially that was the last thing I said before the dismissal, to report anyone acting suspicious."

"And do you think that had an effect on Joseph." He asked

"I would say so, but he had clearly had this on his mind for a while." She replied.

"Please tell us what he told you."

"Well, he approached me after class and said he had something to tell me. I made sure everyone had gone and we had privacy. He then confessed to me that his parents were acting suspicious. I asked him to elaborate and he told me that in public they were normal and agreed with everything he had learned, but he has been sneaking to their room at night and can hear them whisper, and they were talking about either leaving or revolting." Everything was true, but she needed them to act on this to confirm her suspicions and for that she stretched the true a small amount. In all actuality they could be plotting a revolution behind closed doors. The short man had continued writing. Her story was finished, but she could see that the tall man was going to ask her questions. He paused, perhaps pondering his question.

"And have you met his parents?" he asked finally.

"Once, at a conference for the parents." She replied

"And your opinion of them?"

"Well, his father looked very stressed but the mother seemed normal. They both appeared to be in line with common doctrine from my conversation. But then again, things are never what they seem, isn't that right gentlemen?" that had been nearly three months ago now, and she had told the complete truth. In all actuality they both were stressed, she could tell that from her training, but the father showed it while the mother controlled her body much more.

"I see. Do you believe they could be corrupted?" Here was the defining moment of the evening. If she claimed them to be upstanding people and they were not they would be back. On the other hand, if they were not corrupt and she said they were that would also bring them back. This was the moment she made her gamble.

"Without a doubt. I only hope that their corruption will not have an ill effect on Joseph." That was that, she had cast her dice and all she could do was wait.

"Thank you Miss Young." They stood up, the short one rapidly putting away his notepad and pencil. She rose after them. "If we need anything else we will be in touch. Have a nice day." They turned after a short nod and strode out of the room. She sat back down. Tonight she would need to send a report to the mother ship. During the conversation she had collected both voice prints, pictures, and fingerprints but had hacked into the transmission their pollution detectors sent out and captured the digital fingerprint of that signal. They had discovered early on that each detector had a separate and unique identifier associated with it. The mothership was able to track anyone on the face of the planet wearing one and with the code associated to a face her job would be made that much easier. It was oddly puzzling why they had the identifier though, there was no real reason for it to exist. It was clearly placed into the system as a tracking device, they had determined. What they had not determined was who was doing the tracking and why. She knew that tonight had been a breakthrough, they had known intelligence on workers within the system. Now the real work began. She returned to her grading, first things first.

A few days later she was taking attendance when the school administrator came to her class. He apologized for the interruption and handed her a sheet. Joseph would no longer be coming to school. She learned later that his parents had been killed in a robbing attempt late one night. Jan felt a hollow sense of satisfaction and wondered who had done the killing. Whoever it was had been incredibly efficient. She felt herself involuntarily shudder, and the coffee she was drinking no longer made her warm. This was big.

Sam Harrod

It grew like a beast out of control, consuming everything. Sam hated this place and its horribly archaic technology. And now the cell cultures he had hoped would be contained were spreading and eating the chemicals he had theorized would keep them in check. "Oh well" he thought "Maybe if I tweak the glycine content." Sam had never really been cut out to be a spy, he was a first rate scientist. But he had been recruited one day for the program, fresh out of the academy of science, and, in a fit of insanity, had signed up for it. It was duty, he told everyone, but he really yearned for adventure and to see what life was like among the stars. The implications of his actions had not struck him until later, as will the actions of young people. Before long he was struggling through the training, and was ruled out by most of his class as a failure, but he had passed, if barely, and his intelligence had proven to be too good to pass up for the mission and they had plucked him out like a big, juicy ripe grape. He gazed around his cluttered hut. And now he was here. He dumped the compromised cells into a special receptacle he had constructed for biological waste and turned his attention to his work. Biology was not his area of research, but he did keep it as a hobby.

Following the arrival on the green planet he had managed to use his false identity to great effect and now had a cushy semi-high level job in the ministry of green preservation. He was the most experienced agent they had and years of careful study barely kept him out of danger in such a high level post. He had already had to squash two rivalries without giving himself away, which had done adeptly, but knew he gained those enemies through blunders that could have been avoided. He knew he was too absent minded for this sort of job, only his brain kept him out of the fire. He rifled through some reports on his desks, the ministry spared no expense on ministry work so he had stacks of paper usually only used for important documents. Trying to work in research on this planet was beyond frustrating, it was impossible! Two of his research topics had been cancelled yesterday, due to the ill effects they would have on the environment. He hated these rules, and hated the planet even more, but he saw the usefulness in it. Already he had uploaded various technologies previously unknown to the home world that would prove extremely useful. What the green's lacked for in brains they made up in ingenuity, that was certain. To even live on such a desolate place and survive was an enormous feat in and of itself.

The original colonists had somehow managed to find one of the most barren, desolate desert planets in the galaxy, and he would know because he had ranked them as an academy project. Green, ironically, had ended up in 109th place out of 115 habitable planets in this sector of space. 72% of the surface had been pure desert when they arrived, the other 28% a medley of rocky oceans so brackish they would almost kill anything. It was no wonder the terraforming project was attempted so soon after their arrival. They had converted 25% of the desert into lush forest using water trapped deep under the crust. It was enough land to house millions of inhabitants, but green only sported a population numbering in the hundreds of thousands. As a result of the war of restoration the population had split up from the original single city colony and formed pockets of life in the forest, but the main city, Anwe, had remained the most populous. It had also become the headquarters of the ministry of green preservation, the government of Green Planet. Every time he heard that name he chuckled a little bit. The original colonists were so hopped up on drugs they had not even been able to come up with an original name for their new homestead. The balled up the reports of cancelled projects and tossed them into a separate receptacle he used for paper products. Everything was recycled here in Anwe at the large collection and restoration warehouses the original colonists had built. They had pulled apart their space ships and built the massive recycling houses as a testament to their commitment to preserve the life of their planet. If they had used them as actual houses and greenhouses many more would have survived that first year. As it was, the warehouses were the only metal structures anywhere on the surface of the planet. They had been simply known as the "Recycling Center" since their construction to this day. Their capacity had overgrown in years and new structures were in the process of being built to handle the overflow.

He was losing light quickly, as he glanced up the lightning rods running along his ceiling. He pulled out his newest piece of paper, sealed in an envelope, and paused looking at it. This was something completely different than he had seen. It looked...new. It was white, not the dull grey of all the recycled paper everyone used. He turned it over to see something he had not ever expected to see, a wax seal with an odd crest pressed into it. The crest was an oak leaf inscribed with the words "For the good of the world." He broke the seal and opened the envelope. Reaching inside he pulled out a paper of the same quality folded into thirds. He unfolded it and began to read, and as he began to read he began to smile. He had made it.

He immediately took a scan and sent it up to the mother ship with a short attached report. Within minutes he had a reply from the head. It congratulated him on his promotion and authorized additional investigation into the subject. It also came with a warning, from the pieces they had gathered in their relatively short time here they had already started to put together a puzzle of what was going on. Some organization, most likely the government, had access to some other technology to control the population on the planet. Part of that explained the small population, tens of generations had come and gone through the colony and from the original 20,000 colonists slightly over half a million had come of it. It did not fit the population curve whatsoever and the barren and harsh environment was not enough to validate the numbers. They had wondered what was going on since they first scanned the planet and had suspected some form of population control but now they had substantial proof of it going on. The first to go were the non-loyalists, for obvious reasons. The next to go were the ones who had dug too deep, either they stumbled upon something they shouldn't have or they began asking the wrong types of questions in their fervent devotion. The latter were the most dangerous, because they were committed to the preservation of the original intent and swallowed whole the propaganda put out. They even controlled the innovators, persons who had invented and improved the technology without government consent. What they didn't know was how they did it.

And now he had been invited into their ranks. Apparently, bolstered by the recent defeat of his latest enemy, they had chosen him as an initiate. The letter, somewhat nondescript, had advised him only of a time and place of meeting and no other information. But the composition and type of letter gave away, purposefully, who they were. People who could circumnavigate the system, who controlled everything. He had been promoted to the ministry of green preservation administration. Questions with no answers and situations floated through his head now, anticipating the meeting. How would they do it? Was it a trap? He had to be prepared.

He tried working on experiments, he tried analyzing water for pollution content, he tried to test a new device for converting carbon dioxide to energy, he even pulled out an outlandish design for harvesting the power of earthquakes to get his mind off it, but nothing worked. He ended up pacing up and down his lab hut, eager with anticipation. Soon the curfew bells were ringing and he made his way home, to the cozy mansion of a scientist. He was afforded luxuries most would not be; he had a room for every function and none was combined. He had a kitchen, living room, study, bathroom, and bedroom in addition to a foyer. His bathroom contained not only a shower, but a bathtub that wasted so much water when it was filled it would have made most greens flush with anger. And, the most wonderful thing, he had an electric light in his study. It was powered off sunlight gathered during the day so it was not strong, but almost no private homes had them. There wasn't enough sunlight to fully charge his batteries from last nights' research so he left them off and just went to bed.

The next morning he woke to a beautiful sunrise. He saw alone in bed and watched the colors play off his canopy roof, thinking of a life separate from the one he choose, a life of easy and quietness. Sam wondered where he would be if he had not taken this job. Waking up on the home world next to a wife, kids running through the house? Some agents had taken spouses to blend into the local populace, but he knew he could never do it. Soon there mission would be complete and they would leave this planet behind, only to move onto the next one. He had wondered how the others could do it. Many, like himself, remained single and as unattached as they could from the target population. Even though, he still developed friendships and saw the humanity in these people. "They didn't even know that we exist as their enemies, but we are" he thought to himself. He pulled himself out of bed, he had a meeting to be at soon.

He took a shower and used up the last of his stored energy to heat it and ate the last bit of food he had in cold storage. He made a mental note to get more later. He chose the most unassuming outfit he could, a flowing bulky poncho type shirt that went to his knees. It had no sleeves, but the fabric it was made out of was lightweight and durable and kept cold in the summer and warm in the winter. It was spun from a native weed, one of the few gifts the world had provided the unfortunate colonists. The fashion was standard for the day and he knew he could blend in fairly well. He pulled on his pollution detector, took a deep breath, and stepped out his door to walk to his fate.

They had chosen a park right outside the recycling facility to meet him, after the noon bells. He had no trouble getting there and chose an unoccupied bench to sit on. It was a workday so there were fewer people there as usual, only a mother and her child and a few recycling workers taking a lunch break. He saw a runner jog by, an odd sight normally. An old man walked up to his bench and sat down on the far side. Sam continued to watch the action. He enjoyed the sunlight filtering through the trees, looking up and closing his eyes, letting the heat wash across his face.

"It's a beautiful sight, isn't it Mister Harrod." Sam turned to face the man who had spoken. So this was his contact.

"Beautiful indeed Mister..."

"Please, just call me Teacher." The man was watching the young child play in the grass, his mother keeping an eye on him while reading an old book on a bench a way away.

"Yes...Teacher. I find it to be enjoyable." Sam replied, looking back to the garden.

"You might find this life comes at a high cost Mr. Harrod. A high cost indeed. It takes men of stature and will to keep everything in line. Some are fit for the job, most are not. Which are you?" the man had turned to face him. Sam looked back, studying the face, worn with wrinkles. But his eyes gave away the age, deep and filled with experience. Sam felt himself reverting back to his training as he began to become nervous. He slowed his heartbeat and evened his breathing, letting a state of tranquility come over him.

"I love this planet very much Teacher. I would do anything within my power to keep it this way." Sam locked eyes, using his training to show as much sincerity in his voice and face as he could. The man studied him for a long while, then suddenly stood up.

"Very well, come with me. There is much you need to learn." Sam scramble quickly to his feet as the man turned and began walking. Sam caught up with him but the Teacher set a quick pace, one he was surprised at, being the man seem so old. But as Sam studied him he noticed the things underneath the façade. The old man was athletic, his body strong from something. His posture was also extremely good, like the posture of a soldier or someone proud at his job and training. The man did not speak as he led them along a path that wound through the recycling facilities, but soon they were wandering throughout the complexes of the ministry of green preservation, larger buildings at the center of Anwe. Some were built in the early days and the government continued to add and plan to them, each generation of trees forming the groundwork for new buildings. The man led them through paths and road, seemingly intent on leading him some particular place.

"Mister Harrod, what is the very first thing you learn, remember back as far as you can. " the man's words made Sam cautious, but he had done his research of the schooling system and it would have been obvious had he not.

"To protect the environment at all costs." He replied.

"A child's answer to a grownups question." The man said. He stopped abruptly. "I am here to teach you, to be your guide. We are the problem Mister Harrod, we are not the solution. The world will continue as it is, growing and prospering without us. We are but a taint upon it." His words were quite a statement, and completely wrong. The green planet would have continued to be an uninhabitable desert planet had the colonists not come, their presence shaped and improved the land far beyond its natural capacity. Sam gave no indication he disagreed, only posturing his body to display agreement. The man turned and Sam realized they had stopped at a small shack in comparison to the grand buildings around them. "It is time you grew up Mister Harrod." The teacher said as he opened the door. It was dark inside compared to the relative brightness out and the teacher strode through the opening. He had no choice, Sam walked into the gaping mouth of an opening.

He let his eyes adjust to the darkness and let himself gasp in surprise. Here, they were surrounded by metal, a metal box with stairs that led down. He had never seen so much in one place on this planet before, and the Teacher stood directly to the left of the stairs, noting his surprise.

"Yes, we hold the keys to the survival of this planet so we spare no expense in our pursuits. Come, you shall soon learn what we do and how we do it." He turned and began walking down the spiral staircase. "We do not fear technology, we simply reject it as a society. But for that to happen the society must be controlled, led in the right direction." Light was beginning to grow in the stair case, clearly non-natural this far from the surface. The light pipes lost their power after a few feet and became useless. Sam had begun recording from the moment he set out from the door, but he could already sense his connection to the mother ship disappearing from the natural interference of the earth. He kept recording and stored the information for transmission later. The man had continued talking, leading them down into the earth. "This is where we do that, where we use our influence to protect the planet from the common man. We use the resources other cannot, because we are called to a higher vocation. Ah, here we are."

The spiral staircase came to an end the, and led into a short hallway of earth supported by steel girders leading to a steel wall with a large iron door set in the middle. The Teacher walked up to it and knocked. Sam could hear something clicking and shifting and the door began to open. Sam shielded his eyes as light streamed out, much more than his electric light could ever put out. For the second time that day he felt his eyes adjusting and peered into the light silhouetted by the old man. His eyes opened in amazement. He was looking into an access chamber filled with sophisticated electronic security measures and sensors. This type of system was never seen on the green planet, and it looked relatively advanced for the resources they did have. The Teacher motioned him in.

"Please stand on the scanner." He pointed to a glass tube with an opening. Sam stepped inside and the opening closed, the small now-unfamiliar hum of electricity pulsing through the sensors reaching his ears. He quickly activated a shielding program for his suit, something he had not found a need for in his time, making the devices he carried worked into his clothing and body invisible to detection. But as he kept them active he started collecting data on their technology. They were not crude, but neither were they extremely elegant. It appeared they had used the natural ores and materials of the planet to construct them. They were now measuring his biometric information, his heartbeat, body fat percentage, and level of fitness, as well as the toxicity in his skin and organs. A small needle descended from the top of the tube and punctured his skill, taking a sample of his blood. Gas began to filter in from a vent, which his sensors picked up as the vaccine against the mysterious choking disease that afflicted only a few individuals and was always fatal. He breathed it in, and felt a slight tingling in his nose and throat. Air was pumped in through the vent and another at his feet sucked out the remaining vaccine and soon the tube opened once more.

"With this cleansing you have been marked as one of us." The teacher said. Sam stepped out of the chamber. "Now I will take you to the indoctrination room for readjustment." He turned and continued down left, down a white hallway leading away from the access chamber. Doors came and went by as they traveled down the corridor, turning left, then right, then left, until another it ended at another wooden door. This, the Teacher pushed aside, and led the way into the indoctrination room.

It was filled with computer stations, with a different sort of what he was used to and no way like any he had seen. They were made from metal and wood mixed together, with screens of the clearest glass he had seen on the planet. The Teacher pointed to the one closest to the door. There were no others in the room. Sam made his way over and sat in the comfortable chair, waiting for direction.

"We are stretched thin lately. Unfortunately I will not be able to remain with you and teach you, but we have used our resources wisely. You will use this station, called a workbox, to introduce yourself to what you do. I will return in on hour." The Teacher showed him how to use the workbox, and as soon as Sam showed that he could use it well enough, left. Sam did struggle at first, being on a new machine, but he pulled up the files that the Teacher had pointed to and began to read them. He slowly slipped out his own tiny computer hidden in his shoe, careful to avoid detection by the camera he had picked up in his scan. While he was reading the words aloud, like the old man he said, he quietly and smoothly inserted his computer into the terminal. Using the connection to his implanted circuitry he soon discovered he had been invited into the entire wealth of the ministry's knowledge. They kept all their information on the same mainframe, choosing convince over security. He took all of it, continuing to act and speak the words on screen for the microphone they had placed in the room as well. Undetected, he hacked his way through their system and began uploading it all to the mother ship using masks to cover the transmissions. He would have to be gone soon, before they could figure out if anything was wrong or he had taken anything.

Later that night he was ordered off the planet. He faked his own death, using suicide as a cover, and when the team came to pick him up from the rendezvous point, placed a nearly identical copy of him at the scene. It would stand scrutiny to all their tests, but was just a fabricated piece of meat that had never been alive or human.

They took him that first night and began phasing off the other agents. Some were kept long enough to provide for the families they had cared for, but one by one they were removed and shuttled back to the mother ship. They had taken what they came for, and when they were all aboard, the Captain ordered the completion of the report package to be sent back to the home world. They compiled the information for weeks, the entire ship in a panic to reach their deadline, and finally they were done. They sent the information back to the home world and received their new orders.

The Second Planet

The Captain leaned back in his chair, rubbing the sleep from his eyes. A small tone at the door indicated he had a visitor.

"Come in." the executive officer walked in through the self-opening doors. "Ah, I'm glad you're here. I just received the transmission from the home world." The xo had a seat at his desk across from him. "I think you'll find this one quite enjoyable." The Captain handed him the document pad and let him scan it for a few moments, taking a drink of his coffee in the meantime. The executive officer frowned as he read.

"Is this a joke sir?" He asked, looking up from the pad in his hand.

"Absolutely not, that's an order." The Captain replied.

"But our mission is to observe societies, not primitive races." The executive officer said, a slight hint of anger in his voice. The Captain leaned forward.

"Dan, you must not think of it in the way you are. We can't be above anything, it's our job to observe and collect knowledge. Knowledge does not imply technology, rather something greater." He knew if he couldn't convince his right hand man he would never be able to tell anyone else to do it either. "There is something valuable in this planet, it has lasted almost as long as the Common Empire itself. We need to find out why." The executive officer thought for a moment, and the Captain could see the anger being pushed down by something else: curiosity.

"Sir, I'll have the navigator begin to plot a course." He said after a few moments.

"Very well" the captain said with a glint in his eyes, "begin the mission."

Sam Harrod

Blood sprayed through the air and Sam paused to wipe it off his face. Another man came at him from behind, but with his sensors he saw him easily enough and didn't even need the computers recommended swing pattern. He turned and spun his axe upwards, taking off the man's sword hand and cleaving through half his neck. He grimaced as he saw the light go out in his eyes and pulled it free with a horrible sucking sound. Around him men came to his aide, rallying to the banner held by a now veteran banner boy at his side. The tide was turning as the enemy found a rock hard wall where they expected soft underbelly flesh. And here he was, thick in the middle of it. He pondered the irony as he swung at the next man in front of him, axe banging off his shield.

He would have never survived without his computer, setting up algorithms and calculations that analyzed the opponent's movements and revealed their weak spots. It told him where to shore up his own, and where to strike to kill or paralyze. He brought up his shield to match the ghost image of his own in his hand, the computer's way of showing him where to go, and deflected the angry man's sword swipe at his neck. A man to the left of him jabbed his spear underneath the enemies shield arm and a spasm of pain went through his face. Sam swung his axe at just the right angle and took of his head, freeing him from the pain of a punctured lung. The next wave of enemies held back as their line held, and soon they were turning them on their heels, forcing them into a rout. Sam held back as their line surged forward, and let the other men run after, slaughtering the enemy. He only observed now, the battle was over.

He moved among the wounded, calculating the probability of survival and leading the wounded runners to those who had the best chance of survival. They picked up both friend and foe alike under his care, the Castle Corps had proven a valiant enemy and deserved the care and chance at life. Soon the high noon sun had crested the horizon as the last few wounded were moved off the battlefield. The dead caretakers came now, carting off dozens of the bodies to the fires he could smell burning now. He pulled his cloak around his nose and moved toward a copse of trees not affected by the horrible stench. Sam found an unoccupied stump there and looked east out across the field, toward the setting sun. He began to ponder his fate.

In the months he had been on this planet his muscles had grown harder and his body stronger. The wicked looking axe he could barely heft when he arrived had now grown familiar to his grasp, and no longer heavy. He had posed as a beggar when he joined the army, and had looked the part well enough, but with the training his computer had augmented he had rapidly became a trained soldier. He snorted at the thought, a scientist turned soldier. He still had no idea why they had picked him for this one, probably the Captain's bad idea of a joke, but he was still alive, which was no small matter. The Donback people were known for their fighting, but the Castle Corps had risen to meet them in recent years, in both skill and numbers. Fortunately the Donback had the advantage of thousands of years of practice. He shook his head, how did they manage to do it? As far as he could tell they were a well-trained bag of misfits that only enjoyed killing. Well, that and drinking. And also women, but from his research that seemed to be the general trend among soldier no matter what planet or culture. Still, there was something special about them. Numerous rebellions and revolts had occurred, and each time the Donback handily defeated them. They lost their battles occasionally, but they always seemed to win the war. This may be crap but I'm still writing something. He got up and stretched his arms, willing some of the weariness of them. He had to find his unit.

They had promoted him to be in charge of two other soldiers due to his quick advancement in training. Unfortunately one had been killed during the initial charge and the other he had located among the wounded, thankfully only with a broken shield arm and lacerations across his sword arm. He would recover eventually and get back into the fight, the cuts had not severed the tendons like the enemy had intended. He had not seen his leader, or don as they called them, either among the wounded or coming back from the rout. He got back up and picked his way through the now muddy field relatively clear of corpses and headed back to staging area they were supposed to be at before sundown. The sun dipped below the horizon and he heard the wooden drums pounding the call for assembly as the clouds above him were washed in a canvass of reds and yellows.

He entered the main camp and picked his way to the assembly area. Messengers sending reports dodged through out the crowd, and the wounded were still being carried back to the hospital on stretchers of animal hide. As he grew closer to the ring of the great bonfire he began to see more and more familiar faces. He nodded to his superiors, and clasped hands with his training partners, glad to see they had made it. But he did not see anyone, and he saw less than he wanted. He spied the standard of the yellow infantry, and quickly made his way to it. Moments after he had entered their ranks the drums ceased. He found his don, an older man than himself in charge of three low dons, the rank he himself held, and knelt before him to offer his customary report.

"Don Balance, my soldiers, Gabriel and Michael, are taken care of." He began with the customary saying.

"Low Don Harrod, tell me of their needs." Balance look tired, even more so than usual, and blood stained a bandage from his head. He had been in the anvil when the hammer had struck.

"Gabriel has need for nothing." He paused, feeling a wave of sadness and anger come over him. Balance waited for him to continue, hanging his head in sadness with him. Sam went on, controlling his emotions "He has left this world and is cared for."

"May all his days be endless and all his nights be beautiful." Balance murmured. He wrote down something in a small book he had in his hands. "And how fares Michael?"

"Michael has taken a wound, a broken shield arm and cuts to the sword arm. He has treated and taken care of his cuts and has been sent to the doctor for his arm. We should know by tomorrow morning how he fares." Sam watched as Balance wrote again in his notebook.

"Very well. And you, Little Don?" he looked up from his book to study Sam, looking for wounds and pain in his eyes.

"I have only cuts and bruises to bear as trophies, and nothing bad enough to be taken off the roster. I-I feel pain at the loss of Gabriel." Sam said, remembering his follower. They had not been in the same training together, but they were trained at the same time. Gabriel was younger than him, and full of promise. Had he not been a soldier he would have made an outstanding scientist, he was always questioning how things worked and were put together. But there were no scientists here, only soldiers and farmers, and men to rule them. Balance frowned at his words, writing something else in his book.

"It is not wrong to feel such a thing for those you take care of" he said, pulling Sam to his feet "but it was not your fault, whatever you think. You have taken care of him in training and preparation, and his fate is his own. I know you have." Sam felt tears begin to glisten in his eyes, and he realized he had been blaming himself for Gabriel's death. If he had only been there to help him, if he had only stayed close, he could have stopped it. He knew that thinking was futile, and wrong. What happens if he was close enough to save him, would he always be close enough? Balance's words rang in his ears now, and although he did not accept them, he knew he could eventually. Balance saw it in his eyes and nodded gently, his face softening. "Good, you do not have to accept it for now while your grief is strong, but take care of the living while they still are. That is where you will find your atonement. Go, I have your report. Rest easy tonight, for tomorrow will bear its own challenges."

"Tomorrow will bear its own challenges." Sam repeated, feeling the weight in the words. He saluted his Don, closing his shield hand around his sword wrist, and left to find his tent. While he was walking back to in, he felt an urge to go somewhere else come upon him and he was soon at the perimeter of the camp. He saluted the sentries and made his way out of camp, climbing up the slope of a small hill. At the top he stopped, and looked up at the sky. Here, away from all the noise and light of the fires he could make out all the stars in the sky. He slumped down, feeling the weight of his body sink into the soft ground. Here was relatively untouched by the battle and the armies, only showing a few marks where they had marched by to battle. He laid there and watched them twinkle. On the home world there was always too much light and it always drowned out the stars, and they were not allowed outside on the Green planet so he never had the chance to see them there.

They were truly beautiful, and even in space he had never seen more. There were billions, maybe even trillions of them, twinkling and burning in the sky. He wondered which one was the home world, or rather, which one the home world orbited around. He had never been close to his family, but now he found himself thinking about them. He remembered his mother's delicious pies, and his father's soft voice. Gabriel would never see his family again, and he felt something snap inside him. He cried softly, for Gabriel and for himself. He may never see his family again either. For a few minutes he wept silently. He got a control of his emotions and wiped the tears from his eyes, feeling foolish. He was not a child anymore, but now he was weeping like one.

He stayed out there, a blanket of stars, for a few more moments before he contacted the mother ship. There was no technology on this planet for communication, and he was free to transmit any time he needed to. He had recorded the battle, he left his recorders on almost all the time now, and he sent them to the mother ship for analysis. He was still trying to fathom why they needed to be here. Of the technology they had on this planet, the only significant ones worth mentioning were their building and construction abilities. Somehow they had achieved the ability to build grand and wonderful buildings that were incredibly strong and beautiful. Their walls were almost impenetrable, and there were no such things as sieges here. Armies met each other outside their walls, and there was great honor in it. In their time he had only heard of one instance where the defenders of a castle kept inside their walls when the enemy came throughout their history. Their allies came to them and destroyed them all, women and child alike, and handed the city to their enemy on a silver platter. After that he knew of nothing else in their history that would suggest anyone else had done it either. So what was so valuable about this community that needed their attention? He had tried to figure it out from the first day they landed on this very normal planet.

He received confirmation of the upload to the mother ship and stayed on a bit longer, asking for access to the team leader. The operator held him as they went to check for permission, but soon they were back on giving him the go ahead.

"Team Leader this is Agent Sam." He communicated silently in his head. His implanted cybernetics picked up the silent words and translated them into his speech pattern for broadcast.

"Agent Sam, this is Team Leader. Go ahead." He heard the word in his ears but they were audible to him alone, thanks to his hardware package. This way he was able to communicate directly without any suspicion. The only problem was that it took up a lot of power, too much for his energy harvesters to replenish. They had to keep the conversations short when they did happen.

"Yes Team Leader, I am on the ground and in position but require advisement. What should I be doing now at this point?" he heard voices on the end, in hushed tones.

"Agent Sam you are to stay in position and collect knowledge, this was your mission, was it not?" Sam grimaced, of course he knew that was his mission, he wanted to know more than that though. He decided to press his luck.

"Affirmative, I'm looking for more of a concrete answer though Team Leader." This time only a pause before the voice answered again.

"I know Sam." It responded, gently. Like the person at the other end knew how he felt. "Right now all we can give you is that. Carry out the mission."

"Received, Agent out." He cut off the transmission and sighed. Now he was stuck on this backward planet with no idea what was going on and his Team Leader probably didn't know anything either. This was turning into a spectacular day. He checked his battery level, too low. The transmission had taken more than he thought it would. He looked up at the sky one last time, suddenly realized ominous clouds had crept in during his vigil. "Oh great, he thought, there's no way this could get any better." He scrambled up and began to quickly walk back when the first forks of lightning crashed their way through the sky.

He made it back to his tent just as the worst of it arrived. He pulled back the opening and bundled inside the small tarp, soaked to the bone. It never just rained here, it poured. He picked up his pack as water began to seep in under the edge of the tent. He took out a stand from it and set it up. It was designed for this purpose but before the anticipation of battle he hadn't thought to have it ready in case of rain. Thankfully his electronics were waterproof so he lay down on his flimsy cot and listened to the rain pound his thin sheet of a tent. His exhaustion came to him then and his eyes closed, finally feeling the sweet release of sleep take him.

He woke up the next morning to the sound of the breakfast gongs going off. He had slept through the awakening calls, and he scrambled out of bed. He slipped on his axe and strapped his shield to his back and checked his battery levels. About half of what they were last night, the things were working and the energy harvesters were doing their job. He broke through his tent opening, frozen shut from the rain last night and cold this morning, and hurried to the kettles to see if he could get some chow. Luckily he arrived at a food line just as the man before his was getting his share. Sam pulled out a bowl and the cook ladled a fair portion of broth into it, added a chunk of meat from the box beside it and an extremely hard biscuit to top it off. Sam sat down on a log next to the fire and began to eat, enjoying the company of his companions. The meat was gamey, the broth too salty, and a soak in the soup had not softened the biscuit out completely. He had stumbled into the middle of one of Tom's stories, and relished the tale he spun.

"And there, out of the blue, a shield came flying." He spoke, acting out the story to the great amusement of the breakfast club. "And I thought to myself, why waste a good opening, so I turned the direction it came flying out of and there, right in front of my own eyes, I saw Gladdus furiously yanking on his sword handle, trying to pull it free of a man's skull. So then I called out "Gladdus, me boy, this is no time to be dancing with the enemy." Finishing his breakfast and chuckling at his story Sam stood up and walked away, heading to the hospital tent.

It was still bustling, packed with the sick and dying and injured. He noted with sadness how all of them could have been saved on the home world, but medicine was not as advanced here. Men lost arms and legs if they were not treated and the wasting disease took their skin. He could smell it here, the smell of rotting flesh. He shuddered as he made his way through the din, stepping lightly out of the way of the doctors and nurses hurrying to treat the wounded. He looked at their haggard faces and realized that this was their battle, and was just as horrifying and exhausting as the one he had been in. he felt a small twang of sadness for Stan, who would be among them somewhere in the world, and moved on.

He found him in the less seriously injured part of the large collections of tents that made up the hospital. Michael was asleep, both arms bandaged and supports tucked into the right one. Sam kneeled beside him and shook him awake, careful to avoid the bandages. Michael's eyes opened slowly, and they were glazed over.

"Good morning Michael, how do you feel." Michael's eyes were glazed over, and he could tell that someone had given him a large dose of pain killer.

"I'm much better now. Did you know that they broke my shield arm." His words were slurred and he attempted to raise his arm but Sam quickly quieted him and put a hand on his shoulder.

"I did, you fought well yesterday. That's why they were scared of you." Sam said, carefully arranging his arm to sit right. Michaels smiled and then yawned. "You need your rest now, go back to sleep and don't worry about anything." Michael nodded and then closed his eyes and within minutes was sleeping. Sam smiled then, grateful of the life that was in him. He stood and walked over to the nearest nurse, quietly tapping her on the shoulder. She turned, weariness showing in her face.

"Yes dear." She whispered.

"How is he?" he asked, pointing to Michael.

"Oh, he should be fine. We gave him pain killer and he should have a few days' rest, but there was nothing major besides the broken arm and cuts." He thanked her and left, pausing at the door and looking back at his sleeping charge. He was younger than himself, and had just gotten out of training right as they were marching to battle. That had not stopped him from cutting down two enemies before he fell though. And this time, even though Sam was not in the immediate vicinity, his companions had saved him. Luck had been on his side. Sam walked out the door.

The assembly drums had just begun to beat by the time Sam walked up to the staging area. He met up with Don Balance who was already meeting with his two other Little Dons, Little Don Tiger and Little Don Brad. Balance motioned over as soon as he saw him.

"Good you're all here. Any new reports?" he asked

"I just went to see Michael in the hospital tents, he should be fine after he heals." Sam replied, saluting the group. The others saluted him back, respectfully responding.

"Excellent news." Balance scribbled more into his little book. He flipped a few pages in his book. "Tiger you should be at full strength with eight, Brad you lost three so that brings you down to two, and Sam you have only yourself. Our total strength is 14. We should be getting the new recruits as soon as the campaign closes and there should be enough to bring us to full strength." Sam was surprised at the results, even though they did put the better men in the bigger groups.

"Any word on how long that will be?" asked Brad. His eyes looked haggard and he was unkempt. He had lost over half his squad and bore a bandaged hand. Things did not go well for him.

"Well, after the rout of yesterday the Castle Corps split. Their Great Don has been killed so the likelihood of them continuing with the resistance is not high. My guess is they may promote someone else but he will likely crumble the first time they meet us again on the field. For now we need to prepare for that eventuality. No training for the men today, I want them resting after the battle yesterday." The Don looked each of them in the eyes. "And that means you three as well. We'll start up on the drills after that, but we need to keep our strength. Is that understood?" he looked them all in the eyes again, compelling them. They all hesitated.

"Understood." They replied in unison.

"Good." The Don leaned back, satisfied. "The Great Don is pleased with our unit in particular. If we hadn't held they would have been able to divide our forces and we may be facing a different outcome than we are." They puffed up in pride at the compliment, and when they would all go back to their groups they would certainly pass it along. "Now, rest, for tomorrow will bear its own challenges."

"Tomorrow will bear its own challenges." They murmured. They saluted and were dismissed, going back to their own groups. Since Sam had no group to go back to he wandered around the camp for a while. He found himself thinking as he walked, aimlessly going wherever his feet took him. He was dwelling on an upcoming battle when he found himself at the foot of a small rise. Up the rise loomed the headquarters of the Great Don. He blinked in surprise. What had led him here?

He walked up the rise, the place in commotion. Messengers and visitors came and went and he slipped into the stream, attempting to not be noticed. He made it into the entrance and went inside to the message station. Clerks were furiously scribbling at the table and he could see the Great Don and his General Don's consulting. He tuned his equipment to pick up their conversation and found a nook out of the way, trying to stay out of the way. He was able to sort out the voices electronically and focused in on the conversation.

"-advisement is that we strike now, before the Corps can select a leader and while they are still shattered." A testy General said.

"They are scattered, but they are not shattered." Another stepped in. "My scout's report on their condition is pessimistic at best. They were routed, and have dug in on the high ground. If we charge up those slopes in the open our infantry will be decimated before they can even get anywhere." This General was calmer, and collected.

"Yes, but if we strike today then they will not be expecting it." The testy one said. "The advantage of surprise will negate the high ground, if they are in as good a shape as General Don Martinez suggests."

"What the book say?" the Great Don stopped them both, cutting off an argument from General Martinez. Sam could see a man with insignia he did not recognize step forward, carrying a book. He opened it and began to read.

"Two armies, after meeting in battle and-"

"You boy! Answer me." Sam was distracted by a small clerk thrusting a piece of parchment in his face. "Don't you listen? Take this report to the Large Don of the Red Riders on the double." Sam helplessly took it, ears ringing from the interruption of his recorders. The clerk ushered him out of the entrance with a swat. Finding himself outside the tent with an urgent letter in his hands he had no choice. Sam trudged down the slope, mind ablaze with questions about that book. What was it and why had he never seen or heard of it before?

Jan Young

Slowly she pulled the brush down, laying a nearly perfect line of paint in the shadow image her computer had generated for her. It was nearly complete now. She paused and stepped back, looking at her handiwork. A full mural depicting scenes of home life was laid out along the length of the wall, from the celling to the floor. Jan had been excited to take this job, she had always loved painting and now, with the help of her electronics, she had been made one. She was getting better, she knew, and soon she hopes she would have an invitation from the Guild of Artisans. She didn't know what went on in there but she did know that members were the most powerful and influential of nearly anyone except the rulers and warriors. Woodworkers, metalworkers, painters, crafters, artists, they were all accepted into the guild. Anyone that created anything. And the stonemasons were some of the most important within them. She had no idea how they built such amazing buildings, so tall and elegant in this backwards country, but they did. And they kept their secrets too. She stepped back to her work and finished, just as the sun was beginning to kiss the upper edge of the window. Pleased, she picked up her supplies and went to the bathroom to clean her brushes and paint pad.

She packed everything into her pack and stepped out of the bathroom and went down the hall to the entryway. It was gorgeous and she paused at the top of the gold gilded staircase to admire the beauty. The first thing anyone ever noticed was the impressive chandelier, with its millions of tiny crystals dangling like an upside down tree canopy. It took up nearly the entire ceiling, a network of prisms to deflect the light from a small fire set from the room above. It did an adequate job of lighting the room, but that only added to the charm of everything else. The top level was connected to the bottom by two huge quarter circle staircases made of a deep red wood harvested from a tree called the blood tree. Each step had a different scene carved into it, and they all told a story going up or down. The bannisters were gilded with gold and intricately carved into forests of trees with intertwining branches all the way down. In the center of the round room a beautifully crafted fountain giggled and gurgled. At its base were carvings of horses bursting out of the tips of waves, upon them warriors gilded in shining armor supporting a beautiful angel holding a bowl, out of which the water poured. The pink marble of the floor only added to the beauty of the place. She descended the stairs, awed that this was only the house of a common Don, not a high ranking officer in the Army whatsoever. But the man himself had carved the scenes into the steps, and was skilled woodworker. It seemed that when these people weren't killing each other or eating they were making something with their hands.

She exited the grand room and entered the common staircase. This was the center of the building, a high rise built somehow with their primitive technology. She began to descend the square staircase, plain in comparison to the one she had just come from but still ornate.

Climbing down four flights of stairs she found herself in the great lobby of the main hall. Branching off the main room were gardens fed by the light streaming in from enormous glass panels that were pieced together between the four support columns holding up the building. Although the gravity on this planet was less, she was amazed at the height of the building. She walked through the wide streets back to her own building, stopping along the way to buy dinner from a noodle stall down an alleyway. This really was quite an interesting planet if she really saw it for what it was. Suddenly she received a transmission from the mother ship. She gasped in amazement, they were being recalled?

She sent back a query, but it was confirmed. They were being pulled from the planet, for what reason, she did not know. She quickly made it back to her building, pulled a few items from it, and began to make her way to the extraction point. As she exited the city she looked back at its sparkling white walls. It was majestic, the spires of the high-rises pointing up into the sky, almost reaching to heaven. Whatever had happened here on this planet, they were lucky to have such beauty. She shook her head and continued on her way, beginning a long journey on foot.

The stars were out in force and she only had a few hours to sunrise when she made it to the extraction point. It had not made sense to be here in the first place, but now she was wondering why they were leaving. Everyone else had already boarded, she was the last to go. That made her slightly grumpy, but she turned to take one last look at the planet before she climbed into the shuttle. The city was laid out before her in the valley, pinpricks of light complementing the stars. She sighed and boarded the shuttle.

A farmer had risen earlier than intended, his back aching from the planting the day before. He built the fire banked in the hearth and went outside to watch the stars. He was watching the eastern sky, away from the light of the city, when he noticed an odd shape rise from the ground, light on fire, and ascend into the sky. His eyes bulged and he shook his head, murmuring to himself. He focused back on the place he had seen it and blinked. It had gone. Whatever it was, if it had even been there, was gone. "Old boy," He said to himself, "you need to lay off the pipe." He turned and walked back into the house.

Later that day he found himself staring up at the same spot. Days passed and he still wondered what he had seen. Weeks went by and the thought still lingered. He found himself in his field one day, taking a break and looking at the spot, when he noticed a yellow light appear. It seemed to shimmer and sway and the fruit in his hand dropped to the ground. It began to grow larger, and darker. Then it shifted to blue everything ceased to be.

The backwards little world was a small thing, but it made a wonderful sight as it blew apart under the focus of his new little plaything. He smiled, knowing that once again he had purified the universe from another plot of disease and wretchedness.

The Third Planet

What happens now? Dan asked. Silence permeated the air, no one around the conference table wanting to say anything, all of them wondering the same question. The Captain cleared his throat.

"We wait." He said.

"That's it?" Stan asked.

"That's it." The Captain replied. They had their orders, and their orders had been to cancel the watchment.

"Well, shit. I was so close to infiltrating the ruling class too. I'm gonna need a drink." Dan leaned back in his chair dejectedly, folder on the table. They all sat around the table, too stunned to talk. The Captain stood.

"Ladies and Gentlemen, that will conclude the debrief. I would like your reports to the XO by tomorrow morning. You are dismissed." They had taken it as well as he had hoped, an entire year gone by with nothing to show for it. When they had all gone, and only the executive officer remained, he finally broke down and slumped into his seat. "I don't know what is going on number 2." He confessed. "I haven't had word from the home world since the order to abandon the mission."

"Perhaps we should begin exploring?" the executive officer asked. "There are a few systems nearby that may be able to sustain life. At the very least we could determine if they would be suitable for colonization." The executive officer knew the strain that was on the Captain's shoulders, and he knew that the crew was having the same difficulties dealing with the lack of clear and defined mission. The Captain weighed the pros and cons of this idea, carefully turning it over in his head.

"That would work, excellent idea XO. It will get the crew's mind off what's been going on and maybe increase morale a little bit. Have the navigation team find the nearest system and plot a course." The fire began to burn deep inside him again. "Until we go home this ship will have a purpose."

I have no idea what is going on in this book. I seemed to have reach an impasse, what is happening? Is the mission complete? Or doomed? Did a revolt spring out on the home world and now different factions are competing for power? Or is there something more sinister going on?

Stan Super

Bones crunched underfoot as Stan stepped of the final rung of the shuttle access ladder. He looked down and saw the remains of some unfortunate creature under his foot. He gave a start and let go of the runs, falling down the small slope. The others laughed at him as laid there, sprawled out in a comic pose. He checked himself for injuries and was soon caught up in the laughter as he realized nothing was broken but his pride. He got back up and brushed the dust off his clothes and looked around. It was a desert alright. He sighed, imagine, a trained doctor and spy who had mastered any task he set his mind to and now here he was, in the middle of a desert "exploring." Well, it wasn't too bad I guess. He could be stuck on the ship doing nothing like the rest of the crew, but the team had needed a field medic and he volunteered for the job.

The rest of the team exited the shuttle and began to pull out their various scanning equipment. The executive officer led the team, and he kept contact with the Captain using their suits. The XO opened his mouth and began to call them over when a sudden gust of wind came up and blew dust into Stan's face and he stumbled backward against the force, wiping dirt from his eyes. A few of the team members were doing the same, although some had escaped unscathed and the executive officer appeared to be spitting it out.

"Sand-damn. Ok, everyone on me!" the XO called out. They all made their way to him, finding it a little hard to walk in the constantly shifting sand. "They dropped us off at the first set of ruins we found, they're right over the ridge so we're going to go in and analyze them. Now, be careful because we don't know what's down there. Our scans didn't pick up any human life form, but they did pick up a few predators, nothing the zappers can't handle." Stan looked down at his, strapped to his hip. The dull grey piece of metal could be deadly if set to it, but more often than not just used as a way to induce pain and cripple the target. It sent out a huge burst of microwave energy and activated pain sensors in the body. Stan hoped he wouldn't have to use his, he hadn't touched one since the training. "Let's go."

They began trudging up the ridge, feet sinking into sand. It whipped in their faces every once and a while, as if warning them that they were aliens here. They crested the slope and Stan saw the ruins for the first time. They were ruins, much like the pictures he had seen in grade school of ancient civilizations fallen. They seemed made of stone, yellow like the sand itself. Some building shapes could be made out among them, but most were so decrepit it looked as if there were just random patches of stones rising up out of the ground. Whatever this place had been, it was large. The ruins ran into a huge mound of sand, as if there was an entire city hidden underneath. From what they had been able to understand it may be the case. The sand blocked off their scanning signals, and they were only able to detect the ruins due to the odd composition in the sands. And now they were here. The sun was low in the sky but the day already felt warm, he had begun to sweat. The others began the descent down the steeper side of the slope and he followed, sliding down the sandy face. Team members began taking samples of the rock, analyzing the composition and sending the results back to the mother ship. The executive officer called him over.

"Stan, we're going to explore deeper into the ruins. I'd like you around in case something happens." He said, studying a report on his document pad.

"Absolutely sir, I'll stick close." Stan replied.

The XO looked up at him. "It seems as though this area has not seen water in quite some time. The sand here is almost identical to what the stones are made of." He looked into the sky. "It hasn't rained on this planet for quite some time now, and it troubles me. Not a single drop of water in sight." The document pad beeped and the XO looked back down at it. "It looks like we may have found a rabbit hole."

"A rabbit hole sir?" Stan questioned, not quite understanding.

"Oh, it's from something my mother used to tell me. About life on the home world a long time ago. Rabbits were creatures that made a burrow underground, tunneling into the earth. Come with me." The XO turned and led the way through the ruins, picking his way among the rocks and walls. They headed for the great dune and soon they were underneath its shade, standing besides a crumbling building half buried by the sand. A team member stood beside it, scanning the base of a wall. He stood up when they arrived.

"Sir, here it is. There's a cavity behind this wall, and it leads down." Short range scanners had been able to penetrate the sand and stone, but had a much more limited range than the ship's scanners. It also gave a better picture, giving them a better idea what was going on. The scans were sent back to the mother ship and a map was created and pieced together then uploaded to the team. This way they were able to stitch together a map.

"Alright, take us in." the XO responded after a short pause, likely conversing with the Captain sub vocally back on the ship. The team member pulled out a short range laser and activated it, tuned it, and began to cut a hole in the wall. The stone began to heat up with the heat of the laser and the area around the beam turned a bright cherry red. The high power ate away the stone in seconds and within a few minutes he had cut a rectangle into the wall big enough to get a man through bent half over. The XO had called the team and by the time the team member kicked the stone into the blackness they had nearly all been assembled. They lit up their suits, providing an instant light source, and surveyed the room. One section of the far wall had crumbled, and sand had poured into a small mound, but the rest seemed free of the substance. The XO directed a burly man to go in first, one who had been trained as a soldier before the recruitment aboard the ship. He barely squeezed into the hole and disappeared around the corner. His head popped back out after a few seconds.

"It's clear." He said. "I see a small hole in the back though, I'm going to go check it out."

"Acknowledge." The xo replied, "Careful though, I have a bad feeling about this." The man ducked back out of sight and the others started piling in, taking readouts and samples. Stan squeezed in after a few members of the team and found himself in a fairly large room. In the corner a few members were huddled around what looked to be broken jars, furiously testing away. Stan suppressed a giggle at the sight and turned to what the burly team member had talked about. He could see it, a small three foot square hole, most likely an access hole to somewhere. He walked over and peered down it, seeing the rope attached the lip the member had descended on. The light from his suit shifted and moved down the hole, which led into a larger chamber. A strain of curiosity suddenly seizing him, Stan grabbed the rope and began to climb down it. The weight of his own body surprised him as he lowered himself down, and nearly fell off when his feet fell off the wall into oblivion. He jerked his arms and flailed his legs, until he realized he was just a few feet off the ground. He slid down the rest of the way, foolishly, and felt his hands burn on the rope. He looked down at the raw skin, peeled in places from the rope, and reached back with the less injured hand for his pack. He pulled a regenerator from it and gave a few bursts to his skin. The skin grew over the wounds at an accelerated rate and he soon only felt the tingling of pain, an aftereffect from the treatment. If only everything were this easy. His first instinct had been to pull out a bandage, from his time on the last planet, and he realized how much it had affected him.

For the first time Stan looked up at his surroundings. He was in a narrow corridor, with the hole directly above him. The team member before him had left light sticks along his track, leading the only direction away from the rope. He followed the lights, which led deeper down into the earth. He had only gone a few feet when the passageway opened up into a wide circular room. He found the burly team member here, investigating.

"Found anything?" Stan called out. The man paused and looked up from his scanner.

"Nothing worth noting. This place is like a tomb." He said, and returned to his scanner. It was cooler in here, but still quite warm. Sam pulled out his canteen and looked around for somewhere to sit.

He spied an alcove with what looked like a bench and walked over to it. Removing the top of his canteen, he sat down on the stone surface. The room was circular and plain, except for the two alcoves perpendicular to the passageway they had entered from. The other team member was at the other one now studying it. A light dusting of sand covered the floor, and Sam reached down to brush it away. Nothing but plain stone. The whole thing was plain stone, whoever had made this place clearly had no imagination. Sam leaned back into the alcove, resting his back against the cool stone wall. He heard a click. Suddenly, rumbling and the sounds of stone scraping on stone filled the room, and Sam bolted upright with a start, banging his head on the top of the outcropping. The room started to vibrate and he fell to the ground, it was just like one of those earthquakes he had read about when he was a kid. After a time the rumbling and shaking stopped and Stan struggled to his feet, rubbing his throbbing head. He heard groaning and stumbled over to the other man, who was unmoving on the ground. He pulled out his medical scanner and checked the man for injuries. A concussion, but not a whole lot else. Stan felt the bruise on his head and looked up. A chunk of the ceiling had fallen in the earthquake and it appeared to have knocked him on the head.

"XO this is Stan." He sent out a transmission to the team, checking his supplies.

"Do you know what that was?" He received back. Stan confirmed that he didn't have anything that would help the man right now.

"Negative. I have one casualty down here though, concussion. I can't do anything here, he needs to be moved to the ship." Stan replied, sitting back on the ground and finally feeling the effects of being shaken up. His hands were shaking and his legs felt like jelly.

"Roger, we have a few scrapes and bruises but nothing serious here. Where are you?"

"Down that opening we found." Something was nagging at him, like something wasn't right around the area. He felt his body returning to normal and his breathing even. Something caught his eye to the right and he glanced over at it. He took in a sharp breath, not believing his eyes. "You're going to want to come down here sir."

"What is it Stan?" he asked.

"I think I may have just found something." He got to his feet slowly. Where a wall had been now was a staircase, leading down. The curiosity pulled up, and he turned when he heard someone at the rope. He could see their light illuminating down the hole, and the rope swaying back and forth. He turned back toward the staircase and walked slowly and cautiously to it. He pulled a light from his bag and lit it up, pointing it towards the dark hole he had uncovered. It was like an open mouth, leading down into some other world. Sam nervously swallowed as he reached the top stair. He put the light down at the top and pulled out his scanner, turning it on and pointing towards the gaping maw. It led down, farther than his equipment could tell, and was simply a diagonal shaft that cut down at a short 30 degree slope. He slowly took a step, putting his foot on the first stair. He held his breath as his foot made contact and began to gingerly put his weight on it. He eased his whole body and waited for something to happen. When nothing happened, he let out his breath in a sudden whoosh. Nothing had happened.

"Stan!" the sudden noise startled him, and he jumped, losing his footing. He tumbled down the staircase, hitting every jutting edge with his head, until he finally came to rest on a stone floor. Stan groaned, and felt another pang of pain shoot through his head. He had ended up in a heap at the bottom of the staircase and pulled himself into a laying position, various bruises and flares of pain going through his body. He pulled his medical scanner out again and did a sweep of himself. He had sprained an ankle, which explained the pain shooting through that area of his body, and had seriously knocked his head, but he didn't have a concussion. He sighed in relief and felt a couple more pangs shoot up from his ankle. He immediately regretted his curiosity. The XO appeared at the top of the staircase, with a few other members of the team.

"Stan are you alright? You two, take care of him, you come with me." He directed two of the team members away and started down the stairs with another.

"Yes sir, just a little banged up." He tuned his scanner to a pain relief mode and began washing his various bruises and bumps, starting with his head. The pain subsided in his head by the time the XO reached the bottom. He reached out a hand and Stan took it, and he pulled him to his feet. Stan winced at the pain in his ankle, it didn't seem like a bad sprain, but was able to put a little pressure on it. He looked at the XO and realized he was staring at something past him, the same as the other team member, eyes wide in astonishment. Stan turned around to look at what they were staring at and realized why they were so amazed.

They had stumbled into a large cavern, more than three times the height of a normal human. In the center a huge statue stood on a circular pedestal. It was in the shape of a human with wings, but its head was covered by a cowl. It wore a great cloak that obscured all but its hands, one of which was clasped around a great staff with a large hooked blade at the end. Its other hand stretched out, as if reaching for them. It was enormous, its head nearly reaching the ceiling, and the base radiating outward in what seemed to be a ten meter diameter. It was grand, but terrible. A strange feeling came over Stan then, a foreboding that seemed to permeate the chamber. At the base of the pedestal were carvings, what looked to be some sort of language or writing. The XO reached into his pack to pull out a few lights.

"Light it up. Captain, are you seeing this?" the XO handed them the lights and Stand moved to the left of the chamber, placing lights around a square wall. He stopped as soon as he illuminated the first section. On it was carved a scene, a strange carving filled with humans and something else together.

"Yes I am Joe." The Captain's voice filtered through the small microphones on the XO's system. Stan studied the wall, trying to see any sort of pattern. From the staircase side, where he had come from, it depicted normal scenes of life. People eating, people drinking, even some of people in what appeared to be sexual intercourse. As he moved farther from the stairs the scenes became more and more bizarre. Images of war, killings, kings on thrones and mountains of treasures, even one of what appeared to be a thief, stealing from the rich man. But that was not all, Stan moved farther and farther away. When he reached the base of the statue the images turned to death and torture. Filled tombs and coffins gave way to strange creatures and men in pain, fire and ice licking at their bodies. The beings had horns and sharp teeth, and almost looked like humans if their faces hadn't been twisted into snarling features and their bodies as well. They stabbed and cut humans, whipped them and pulled them apart. The images were disturbingly grisly and Stan found himself unable to look anymore. He had reached the end of the wall and carving and when he turned away from it he found himself staring at a great room of darkness, even larger than the one they were in. Dividers of stone ran along the room, parallel to where he was looking. He looked down and saw another staircase leading down, this set not quite as steep and only a few steps down.

The XO had followed them around the statue and was standing still, looking out at the cavern. He descended the few steps and was at the base of a divider, about the width of two people lying side by side. The cavern was natural, not constructed, but whoever had built this place had adapted it to their purposes. The air was cool and dry, but it was not cold. Gravel crunched underfoot, and Stan looked down to find a thin layer of it covering the cut stone. "Odd," he thought to himself "what's the reason for this?" the other team member joined them at the base of one of the dividers, which were about the height of two people.

"What are those things?" The Captains voice asked, disembodied in the still air. The XO pulled out his scanner and swept over the stone pillar. He stared at the scanner, then moved to a different position. He scanned the thing once more and looked up from his readout.

"They're holding bodies. We're in a crypt."

It turned out that they didn't get a chance to learn more about the ruins. Stan shook his head, taking another sip of coffee and staring out the porthole towards the alien planet. Whoever had been there, they had all died long ago. The planet itself was dead now, so dry that nothing was able to grow on it. It was now a barren land of sand and rock, the entire ecosystem gone. It had turned into a cursed planet, and Stan wondered how much of that curse affected him. Turning away from the depressing, yet beautiful sight, he returned to his seat with the other crewmembers.

"Was is that bad?" Sam asked, looking questioningly into his eyes. Stan looked back, holding his gaze. He adverted his eyes to the deck of cards on the table and picked them up, beginning to shuffle. Silence gripped their table as they all waited for his answer.

"I don't know. I don't know what happened down there or why, but something was wrong. Planets aren't made to die out like that. It was unnatural." Chills ran down his spine at the memory, his mind wandering back to the look on the dead man's face. "And it was protected." He had somehow triggered a trap trying to open one of the coffins, and an unknown gas had poured of the opening. The man's scream still echoed through his mind. Sam reached over and clapped his shoulder.

"It wasn't your fault, no one could have known they had booby-trapped the place." Sam said in a calm, reassuring voice. "Believe me, I know what you're going through." Stan looked up, back into his eyes, and saw the weight of his words.

"I just wish I could have saved him." Crewman Robert Lestraude. That name would be burned into his memory forever. He had opened the crypt, and it was his fault that man was dead. Stan felt some measure of comfort from Sam's words, but the weight of his actions still hung heavy around his neck.

The Fourth Planet

The Captain sat back in his chair. They had finally received their orders, and this time it was serious. He knew that part of the reason they had been receiving easy assignments was to train them, but now it seemed the training wheels were off. He pulled out two cigars from his secret stash, and clipped off the ends. He paged the XO and waited, pouring a glass of fine scotch for himself. Minutes later the XO had arrived and the Captain called him in when the door chimed.

"Pull up a chair Joe." The Captain said, motioning towards the empty chair across from him. The XO sat, aware of what was about to happen. He had done his research on the Captain before he arrived with the ship, and he knew he was a traditionalist. Cigars meant one of two things to him, that they had just survived something they shouldn't have victoriously, or they were going into the situation. He accepted the cigar and lit it from the pack of matches the Captain had procured. They let the quiet linger, enjoying the quality of the tobacco. These were fine cigars, holdouts of the old ways, and could rarely be found anymore. They both followed the smoke as it wafted and curled around the room, escaping out a vent to be purified through the ships systems.

"It's bad, isn't it?" Joe asked. The Captain took a long draw on his cigar, the end growing cherry red with the burning. He blew out a series of perfect smoke rings and let the rest escape from his mouth. He slid the data pad across the table, which the XO picked up and began reading. Joe whistled softly. "Well I guess we finally get to cut our teeth." He said, a sad chuckle escaping him.

"It's not completely hopeless, not yet. We have two months to train for this, so let's get it right." The Captain said.

"I'll draw up the plan immediately. We're going to have to have something spectacular for this to work." The XO attached his document pad to the device and transferred the material he was allowed access to. They sat together, enjoying the rest of the cigar and the Captain poured the XO a drink. Wordlessly they finished, and like they were both in a daze, they stood. The XO saluted and the Captain returned it. He spoke then, with all the confidence of a man prepared for death.

"Let's give them a show, shall we?" They both grinned, partly from the booze and partly from the anticipation.

Dan Reich

Dan shuffled through his folders, trying to find his notes on string theory harmonics. He was exasperated by the technology on this planet, and was having a hard time adjusting. He flicked through his recent messages, trying to find the file he needed. "I'm sure the professor sent it out yesterday, or was it Monday?" he thought to himself. After five more minutes of searching he finally just threw his hands up and walked out of the interaction room. He stalked over to his food module and slammed the quickset for coffee. The advanced device spit out a stream into his favorite mug and he grabbed it, sending hot coffee spraying all over the interface and on his hand.

"Damn it all!" he yelled, switching his mug to his other hand to suck on his burnt hand. He reached over to the medical cabinet and pulled out the treatment wand. He set the mug down on the table, gingerly this time, and waved the wand over his hand. Immediately the skin began knitting up and the pain subsided, replaced by the unusual tingling the device always seemed to bring. He was exhausted, exasperated, and angry. When they got the mission no one thought they could successfully plant agents on the planet Barkbeat planet, but with some ingenious work by the Captain and his crew they were able to slip in unnoticed and take up residence under the authorities' noses. That hadn't made life any easier for him though. Now, he found himself back at school. As a grown man and trained spy, nonetheless! None of that actually bothered him though, it was the difficulty at which he had trying to remember all the material. He was not a stupid man, he had graduated top of his class during training which had led them to select him for this mission, but things were not coming as easily as he remembered them. Now it was all engineering and science and string theory and paramagnetism and nanobots and millions of things he hadn't even heard of, particle replication and quantum hysteresis. He was going insane. He slumped into the chair, letting his body conform to the ergonomic back. But worst of all, he was lonely.

It had been three months since they dropped him off on the rock, and he was amazed at some of the stuff they had. Humans had been able to expand their lifetimes tenfold, and now sometimes lived a full century. The greater gravity had forced their bodies into more squat forms, and as short as he was, he was still considered tall here. But there medicine was incredibly advanced. New forms of disease developed constantly, but they were able to nullify the effects within years, somehow they had been able to tap into the human body itself and found ways of growing back lost limbs, decayed brain cells, almost anything. Now, when people got hurt, it was seldom life threatening. It was all mysterious to him, but that wasn't his area of focus.

No, Dan was after a far juicier prize. They had developed some sort of teleportation device and were able to go almost anywhere they wanted on the planet. Each house or apartment had its own travelling room, as they called them, which were connected in a large web all over the planet. All you had to do was input your destination, get in, and then wait for the other end to clear and it would whisk you away and in milliseconds you would be standing at your destination. And here he was, trying to study to become a travelling technician, one of the people assigned to provide maintenance to the teleportation chambers. The only problem being that these things were fiendishly complicated. From his basic introductory classes he learned that somehow these devices cut a wormhole directly between the two ports. That boggled his mind when he first learned that, from his understanding of wormholes. But from his later, and more advanced, courses he had learned that was just an oversimplification. He still didn't understand what was going on though. They hadn't been able to make regular transmissions to the mother ship, he had been very careful to mask his transmissions and always hopped locations. He didn't know how he was going to finish this, he had gotten pretty poor marks all along the way and the future was not looking bright for his mechanical career. He still had passed everything though, if by the skin of his teeth. "Only two more months" he told himself "And I'll be out there learning the trade and hopefully unlocking some secrets." What he had uploaded had helped out tremendously, if it was only basic texts and materials. He had scoured the school library for anything else he could use, but the sheer volume of the materials proved to be too hard of a task and he just tried to dump as much as he could and send it up. Right now, though, he needed a change of pace. He put on a jacket and grabbed his hat and went over to the transportation room. He got inside and closed his eyes, and randomly punched the keypad, activating the device. He heard it activate and he opened his eyes, seeing what random chance had got him. The room hummed and he felt the tingle of energy running through him and suddenly the lights flickered and he was in a larger teleportation room. He stepped out of the room, although it didn't look like there was a huge demand for the thing and stepped into a room. He scratched his hat, peering around the place. He smiled in disbelief, then began to laugh. The waves of laughter washed over him, coming from deep inside of him, washing away the stress from his body. He kept laughing, he fell down, and he laughed until he cried. Eventually his mirth began to subside and he recovered from it. He opened his eyes and saw an old lady standing over him, a suspicious look on her face.

"Can I help you sonny?" she asked. She did not seem amused. Her withering look sobered him and he quickly got back up on his feet.

"Oh, yes—where am I?" he replied, brushing the dust of the floor off his pants, "other than being in a barn, that is." He chuckled again, a barn.

"That would be Halfacre Farms young man." Dan was slightly taken aback, but then realized the average age was so much longer here that meant he probably was a youngster to most.

"Ah, is it closed?" he asked. Her face split into a smile then, her wrinkles cracking with mirth.

"Closed, come on." She said as she turned, motioning him to follow. "Clearly, you don't know anything about farms." She chuckled and he heard her mutter "closed" and snort. He followed here and looked around. This was most certainly a barn, the travelling chamber opened into the main room and stalls filled the walls. Up overhead half a floor jutted out from the far wall with a ladder leading up to it. It was covered with hay. Animals filled the stall, strange beings that he had never seen before. They made odd noises he had never heard before. The lady led them out through two large doors and he followed. He stepped aside as she shut them and swung a latch to lock them. The sun was just above the horizon here, morning here when he had just come from evening. Where ever this place was, it was halfway across the world. The lady led him to a small house and opened the door.

"Now I know you must be hungry so I'll feed you, but we'll need your help in the fields." She walked into a small kitchen and he followed apprehensively, what was she talking about? "I've got bacon and eggs and some toast with fresh milk if you want that." She began opening cupboards, pulling down plates and silverware.

"Excuse me for a second, what did you mean about the fields, and why are you feeding me?" he asked, standing in the doorway. She stared at him for a moment before continuing here arrangements, setting everything at a table tucked away in the corner.

"Well you're at the Half Acre Farms, I'm assuming you want the farm experience, yes?" she paused again, table set and arranged for one. He had no idea what she was talking about, but this was a change of pace.

"Oh, absolutely." He replied

"Good, breakfast and lunch and you'll work for two hours in between, unless you don't like the agreement?" she raised an eyebrow, as if she was daring him to argue.

"No, no, that should be fine." He surrendered himself to chance once again.

"Good, now sit down." She went to work, cracking two round things and pouring out their centers onto a dish shaped bowl with a handle. She reached into a white box and pulled out a container of milk and a brown package. He sat down at the table, covered in a checkered cloth pattern, and stared down at the plate. On it was a painting of a large bird looking back over its shoulder at smaller birds following it through long grass. How odd. Dan looked back up and studied the room, it wasn't very big, that's the first thing he noticed about it. It also had none of the technology he had come to expect. There was no food module, only the large white box and a metal one the lady was at now, the one she had put the bowl on. He could tell it was heating up whatever she was doing, and wonderful smells began to fill the air.

"What's your name dear?" She asked, busily stirring whatever she was doing.

"Ah, I'm sorry, I'm Dan. It's a pleasure to meet you." He said. "Please excuse my manners."

"No, no, it's fine" she said, "My name is Sally and I've met a few people with worse manners than you." The bowl was making a lovely crackling and hissing noise and she turned around and slapped a steaming pile of food onto his plate, which he recognized as eggs and bacon. She poured him a tall glass of milk and continued talking. "Here you go, this should fix you up just right. I apologize for the butter, we had to make a new batch this morning and it's not quite done yet." Dan stared at his plate, smelling the wonderful aroma coming off the plate. Sally noticed him staring and urged him on. "Go on then, take a bite and tell me how it is." He picked up his fork and loaded it with eggs. It looked differently than what eh food modules produced, but he decided to go for it. He closed his eyes and put it into his mouth.

As he chewed he tasted the wonderfully cooked eggs, still hot from the pan and felt his mouth instantly salivate. He picked up a piece of bacon and bit into it. It was crispy, but at the same time it was soft, a most wonderful contradiction. He decided to try the milk then, ignoring the layer of bubbles that had formed and let the fluid rush into his mouth. His taste buds were on fire with goodness, this had to be one of the best meals he had ever eaten in his whole life! He pulled himself away long enough to notice that Sally had sat down across from him, seemingly still waiting for a response.

"Wonderful," he choked out between bites, "It's all wonderful, more than wonderful. This is amazing, how did you do it?" he questioned. She chuckled.

"Well now, if I gave up my secrets that easily they wouldn't be secrets, now would they?" She watched him devour the meal. "Thank you for the compliment though, most people don't like what I fix for them. And by most people I mean my husband if you were thinkin' of askin'." Within minutes the food was gone and Dan was completely satisfied, no thoughts of his mission in his head. "Well, well, " she said "it seems you have quite an appetite. I'll have to remember that for lunch."

"Thank you so much for that." Dan said, leaning back on his chair and patting his belly. "I really don't think I've had anything like that in my life."

"Well don't be thanking me just yet." She said, getting up from the table, "From our arrangement you still have some time to put in, and I reckon you won't find it quite as enjoyable as this. That's the downside of life, with the good comes the bad." She collected his now empty plate and glass and brought them over to the counter, opening a door and pulling out a rack. She placed the dirty dishes in it and closed it back up. "I suspect my husband will be back soon and he'll fetch you right out." She gazed out the window, searching for something.

"There he is now, on your feet." Dan got up out of the chair and followed the old lady, who had gone out the door they had come in.

Sam Harrod

"They set me up with a cushy gig this time," he thought to himself as he poured a glass of firewater. He chuckled at his situation. Somehow a spy had found work as a private investigator. Somehow. He was running low on cases, but that just allowed him to investigate things that would prove useful to the home world. He went over his list of dossiers as he leaned back in his comfy chair. That was one thing he always did enjoy, comfortable chairs. It was almost a staple to thinking well. Right now he was working on a human trafficking case. Organized crime on this planet was very organized. He had uncovered the first criminal company on accident the first time. A lady had hired him to spy on her husband, thinking he was unfaithful. Well, it turns out he was but it also turned out he was a lesser ranking officer in a drug ring. Most narcotics were legal but some manufactured drugs were extremely dangerous and addicting, and were consequently outlawed. The ring he had stumbled into had dealt an extremely potent version of painkiller called the Minderaser. It essentially shut off every nerve in the human body, cutting off all feeling, and induced an extreme euphoria. From there came the hallucinations, and a huge increase in energy and strength. Users had to lock themselves away from the world, often strapping themselves up and away from anything that could possibly hurt them. The ones that didn't usually were found dead, oftentimes jumping out of a window by accident. Sam had been able to stay out of the way and they never noticed him, but they were clearly hardened criminals. They got rich off the substance, building huge palaces and indulging in every whim they wanted to, but were rarely caught. They had actually led him to the human trafficking ring.

A few of the gang members were actually working for both rings. The traffickers found out and didn't think that was such a good thing so the two double sided men had ended up losing their lives. It was far easier to dispose of bodies with their technology, and there had been an investigation but the cops had turned up nothing. He still didn't have the contacts he needed within the police force, but he was steadily working on it and had established a few relationships catching a couple fugitives a few months back. Mostly he did investigations for private customers, but he had needed the money on that one and work was scarce. The upside to this planet was the digital records and networked computer system. Sam had been able to hack into that within a few weeks and modify some records with the help of the mothership. Now all the agents had digital histories, all orphans who grew up on the streets and were now working their way steadily up through society. At least, that's how it would look to the average and even trained individuals who wanted to know anything about them.

He dropped the dossiers back onto his desk and got up. He paced around the room for a while, then went to the sanitation room. He had lucked out and found an old apartment to work out of, it still had an archaic water cleansing station. He had grown fond of them during his time on the Green planet and had missed them dearly during his stint as a soldier. His muscles still held their strength, he had been practicing with the old training drills he had learned in addition to the newer weapons. He let the water pour over him, feeling the heat transfer to his body. The temperature was almost unbearable, and by the time he exited the station he was red from it. He dried off and threw on a change of clothes. On a whim he grabbed his hat and headed out the door. He wasn't sure where he was headed, but his instincts always led him somewhere. He climbed down the stairs, his building was ancient after all, and entered the main lobby. He waved to the doorman, who doubled as the maintenance man, and pushed his way into the cool breeze of the night.

He turned left, towards the city, and started walking. The lights of the city drew him like a moth, enticing him. He hopped into an empty transit pod and lay back, selecting a random building within the city. The thing hummed to life and he began to move along the tracks. The sky was washed out here, just a blanket of black and a couple of moons that orbited the planet, and was nothing like the skies he had seen throughout his travels. Looking up at it brought back memories though, the pain and sadness welling up inside him. He had yet to come to terms with it completely, but he was recovering. Building tops rushed by, growing larger and obscuring more and more of the sky as he grew closer to the heart of the city. He knew he would have no problems with traffic, almost everyone used the teleportation system to get around, including himself, and he soon found the pod slowing down. He sat back up and looked around. He recognized the place only as the southeastern corner of downtown, and he didn't recognize any of the landmarks he got out of the transit pod and paid his money. The way they did it here was to take a fingerprint and charge your bank account directly. Or what they used to call bank accounts, since there was no real supply or hard supply of money, finding a place to store it was no longer part of anything. Now they just used loan companies to handle the movement of funds and you could "store" your money in an imaginary vault that existed somewhere within a government database. It was handy for them since Sam was able to hack into that system too. Now, they didn't really need money, but they had to be extremely careful about the trail he left or someone would get suspicious. So they generally just made their own money, preferring to use that instead.

Sam walked around downtown, through all the lights and glamour of the storefronts. People still liked to window shop here, and even though they could teleport right into the stores they generally didn't. So he found himself walking along with the crowd. His mind kept coming back to that night, and those words. And then to the image of the mess, talking with Stan and seeing his pain and anguish. A light rain began to drizzle down, and he raised his face to it. The Don had been right, it really wasn't his fault. He felt something snap inside him, and it was if a weight was lifted off his chest. He didn't realized how much that death had affected him until now, and as he stood there in the rain in the middle of the crowd he felt as if a sickness was being washed away, a thin layer of grime and dirt, down and into the gutters. He felt relieved, and he knew that soon nothing else would matter here. As soon as this mission was complete they should be going home. He longed to see his family once more, the family he hadn't been close to but still was his. He had finally forgiven himself.

Jan Young

She trudged through the rain back to her apartment, umbrella held overhead to fend off the water. Rain was all well and good, but it never rained when she wanted now did it? Today, however, it reflected her mood: fed up and gloomy. She hated this new job, especially because no one listened to her. She had picked up a clerk job at the local records department, a government job, but it was not going well. Every day she dealt with unruly mobs of people who refused to stand in line like they were supposed to and always demanded service right away without realizing how much work actually needed to be done. People applying for permits, people applying for licenses, people wanting to sign a marriage certificate, the list went on and on. She splashed through the puddles building up, not caring where the water went. She got a few angry replies as the water hit some around here, but she really didn't care. All she wanted to do was go home and get out of her wet clothes.

When she had finally made it and got dry and clean, her mood had lightened considerably. It may have been due to the fact she was going to enjoy doing her real job for once, but it was more about the fact she could control something for the first time today. Jan got a nice warm cup of coffee and curled up in her favorite chair and settled down for the task at hand. She pulled up the information she wanted in her interactive room and began to set the encryption procedures to work. As soon as they were finished she would be able to dig around within the government system looking for clues and knowledge. It took a few moments to set the proper procedures in place, but with that out the way she rolled up her sleeves and got down to business. Sam had been able to hack into the government systems and the rest of the team had been relayed the information from the mothership so she knew had to slip in under the system, and proceeded to do so.

As soon as she was in she went straight for her target. The Barkbeat natives had been advanced in their organic shipbuilding technology for a while now, and they far outstripped the Empire in that regard. Jan infiltrated the military records and reports, looking for the latest secrets and downloading them to her secret cache. She wouldn't be able to upload them to the mother ship right away; they needed to be more cautious than that. While snooping through the latest reports she discovered that the military was planning on building another class of supply freighter, which she stored in the mundane, had taken a few casualties in a skirmish with space pirates, a little bit more interesting, and then something caught her eye. Her hands trembled and the coffee mug fell out of her hands and shattered on the floor. A report raised concerns the Empire may have spies on the planet, and detailed how a ship designed for the purpose of espionage had slipped out of Gemini Conglomeration hands and observation days after it had left port. They had tracked it to the two planets they had already been to, Green and Rumblebeat, with the dates of discovery on each. They had left Rumblebeat only days before the Gemini Conglomeration had tracked them there. And now they knew they were here. This was bad. Jan downloaded the document and immediately cut the link to the database, checking her security measures and scrambling the code just in case. She sat back in her chair, her mind awash in doubts and scenarios. What was she going to do? Somehow she needed to get in contact with the mother ship, but her next scheduled rendezvous wasn't for another two days. If she waited that long the Gemini Conglomeration's counterspies could have tracked them down and the entire mission would be a failure.

She got up and paced around the room. Clearly, she had to get in contact, but she needed a secure location to do so and now she wasn't sure anything was secure anymore. She had no way of getting in contact with the others, and there was no way she would now. If any one of their covers were blown it could put them all at risk. She slowed her pacing and began to practice breathing exercises she had learned in basic training. She lay down on the floor, face down, and began to calm herself. Whatever she was going to do had to be calm and collected, otherwise she was as good as dead, she knew that for certain. As her thoughts slowed down and the panic drifted away from her mind she began to formulate a plan. She would have to find a secure location and send an emergency beacon to the mother ship if they were ever going to get away. That would be the first step. She got back to her feet, calmed down, and looked outside to see the rain had not let up during the evening and now the sky was dark with night in addition to rain. She pulled her umbrella back out, coded the message, and them began to scan the city map for someplace unobtrusive but not obvious, and not somewhere that would give her away easily. She settled on finding somewhere mildly crowded with little or no surveillance: the midnight bazaar.

She knew she had made the right choice when she stepped into the bustling alleyway. Noise filled her ears and smells assaulted her, from the various market stalls scattered throughout the place. She strolled casually through the market, pausing at stalls occasionally. Jan was checking for followers at every turn, and subtlety masking her scans. If she tried to leave a beacon someone might find it and begin to trace it back to them, or it would at least confirm their presence here. She checked once more around her for followers and sent off the transmission, letting them know she would be able to receive for a few more minutes while she was still in the bazaar. The crowd pushed around her, struggling to flow in both directions in the middle while the edges were stopped at the stalls. She felt herself being taken along with them and stepped out of the way, finding herself in a stand.

The stalls were sectioned off with small metal bars as walls, and she had found herself in a rug salesman's store. He was situated at the back, flipping through an old fashioned magazine and ignoring his customers. Two others occupied the stall, two women babbling over the rugs and gossiping about each other's lives. Jan casually walked closer to the inside, feeling the weave on a rug hanging from the wall. They were good quality, probably knock offs, and some of them were very beautiful. All of them were designs of shapes; none had images of daily life or people bathing. The fabric felt good between her fingers and she paused to admire it, forgetting for an instant about her dilemma. A message buzzed in her head then, causing her to jump in surprise. She calmly collected herself, and exited the stall, nodding at the salesman, still engrossed in his reading.

As she walked along, pausing occasionally at a stall to look at the merchandise, she checked the message. She had been advised to gather what she could within a few days, and soon she would be extracted. Jan half smiled to herself, and although it left a bitter taste in her mouth, she relished the thought of being free from her frustrating daily job. She felt eyes on the back of her and something nagged her intuition. She stealthily held up a bright polished metal bowl in the light, pretending to be studying it. In the reflection she could see the crowd, and she spied a man staring at her. She bought the bowl, haggling with the merchant to avoid suspicion and turned around. The man was still there, slouched up against a market support, but he was no longer looking at her. She turned and made her way down the crowd, passing a few stalls before coming to rest on one that sold beaded trinkets. She used a cloaked scan on the crowd, and picked the man up. So he was following her. A chill ran down her spine as situations ran through her mind. She knew that there would be no good end to this outcome. She quickly ran through possible escape situations and settled on the thing she knew would work.

She began to walk again, attempting to spy a good place to do it. She saw an alley down the street a little ways and began to make her way towards it, occasionally stopping by stalls to avoid suspicion. She turned down the alley, using an internal map for direction, and began to walk down it. It was a side street, and made a few turns before it exited back onto a major thoroughfare of the city. Jan noted that the man had turned down the alley behind her and she prepared herself. He caught up to her at the first bend and grabbed her arm.

"Hey babe, where's a pretty thing like you going? This alley isn't a place you should be." The deep, husky voice said. Jan stopped and turned around to face her follower for the first time. As soon as she leveled her gaze at him he dropped eye contact and her arm, nervously shuffling his feet around.

"What do you want?" Jan demanded. He looked back up and opened his mouth. Then he closed it again as he raised his hand to scratch his head. He opened his mouth again, and finally began to speak.

"Well, um, I was – I saw you at the rug place and had to come talk to you." He stuttered out. Jan stared at him. "Are you doing anything? I could pay for coffee if you wanted to—" he cut off as he realized she was just staring at him. She searched his eyes, and then began to realize what was happening. He was slightly unkempt, and his posture horrible, with what appeared to be a gut in his belly. His muscles were not hard, and the look in his eyes said he was soft. She began to relax, and suddenly she was laughing. The man blinked in surprise, taken back by her response.

"No, honey, I'm sorry. I'm already taken." She said, mildly amused.

"Oh." Was all the man said, clearly dejected. He turned back toward where he came, walking away with his head hanging. Jan slumped up against the wall and smiled. She slid the knife back into her sheath. She was prepared for anything. Here she was, thinking she had a tail by the Gemini Conglomeration and it had been a horny man looking for a night of heat and sweat. Her plan had been to kill him, and she was glad something had held her back. A body in an alley was no way stealthy at all. Bodies tended to bring investigations, and investigations were the last thing she wanted. Relieved, she continued down the alley until the main street. She found a small little coffee shop and grabbed a cup of hot chocolate before she used their teleporter to go back to her house.

She was sitting at the kitchen table when she heard a knock at her door. Wondering who it could be she went over to answer it. Before she could reach it the door flew at her, slamming into her, and she fell to the ground. The last thing she saw before everything went dark were the shapes of people moving into her apartment.

The Fifth Planet

"This is the Captain speaking. I have received word from headquarters that our replacement crew is not trained yet and our deployment has been extended by another year. I know that many of you are anxious to get home, but we won't be back for a while. Everyone is allowed one thirty minute message to send back to whomever they want so prepare your words. Captain out." The Captain turned off the microphone and looked around the bridge. A stunned silence permeated the air, and he could see the shock in the crew's faces. John Smith, the weapons officer sat down in his chair like he had been punched. Having said what needed to be said the Captain rose from his chair. The depression was too much, and he turned the microphone back on.

"This is the Captain speaking. I know what some of you are feeling." He said, forcing eye contact with the bridge crew, one by one. "And I know personally how hard it can be. But I promise you this, I will do everything, everything, within my power to get this ship home safely. If I have to use my dying breath to issue that command to return home, I would do it in a heartbeat. So please stay with me, we have made it this far." The last eyes he met were Officer Smiths, and he saw a faint glimmer of hope in his face as he nodded. "Captain out." This time there was a steely determination in the air, a resolve to keep fighting no matter the costs. The Captain descended the stairs and made his way to the passageway to his chambers, patting arms and shoulders along the way. He made it off the bridge and into his chambers and fell into his chair. He pulled the locket out from underneath his uniform and opened it. "I wish I had the resolve I told them I did." He whispered quietly to himself. He ran a finger along the edge of the picture, remembering her touch. The door beeped softly, interrupting his reverie. He closed the locket with a snap and returned it to his hiding place. "Enter" he commanded.

The doors slid open and the XO stepped through them, face overcast from the news.

"A year?" he asked. The Captain motioned him in to sit and made sure the door was closed before he gave his response

"That's an optimistic estimate. There was a training accident with the replacement crew, headquarters suspect sabotage, and they're scrambling to find new recruits. Whoever they are, they're going to be the second hand pick so it will probably take longer to train them. We may be looking at two years if things go poorly." The XO's face darkened even more. This was bad news.

"And now the Gemini Conglomeration knows about us and is tracking us." The XO said angrily.

"Yes." The Captain replied, softly. It was a small wonder they had escaped with the team from Barkbeat. They had moved instantly when they had the information from Agent White, and had managed to get away with much more than they had originally anticipated thanks to the work of the field agents. But it had been close; they had narrowly avoided a Conglomerate light cruiser in their escape and had to jump multiple times before their beacon was lost. "And that's where the main problem lies. I think there may be a spy aboard the ship." The XO's face turned from dark to surprise in an instant.

"A mole?" he asked.

"I know we have one somewhere, and they may be on this ship. They could also be at headquarters, but my instinct tells me they're here." The Captain had been careful. The first time he suspected he had done a careful analysis of the XO's comings and goings, and of all his transmissions. He was as clean as he could tell, although he was caught up with some sort of relationship with a lesser crewmember. The Captain had locked the door and conducted a sweep of his quarters, discovering a small bug in his chambers. He pulled it out now and laid it on the table. The XO looked down at the device, not recognizing it for anything. "It's a bug, a small recording device. I don't know how long it's been here but I've been jamming it with music and false conversations for a while. I need it analyzed by someone I can trust." The XO looked back at him. "Joe." The Captain said softly "you will cut off all contact with Crewman Norales immediately. If I catch wind of anything like it again I'll bust you so hard you'll be happy to clean out the purification conduits." The XO dropped his head, a blush coming to his cheeks.

"I hadn't meant for anything to happen." He said.

"I know, but its time you started acting like the Executive Officer and the second in command." The Captain replied. A silence hung between them, a small measure of trust gone. He knew that it would not be exactly the same, but he had to do it and he knew Joe well enough to know he would heal and earn his trust back.

"I know you had to Captain, and I knew I needed to stop, but I'm not the spy." The XO said finally, looking up from his shoes. The Captain nodded.

"I trusted you before; I just needed to verify it. I need you to do the same for me."

"What? Investigate you?" he asked, slightly shocked.

"Yes, if I investigate this crew I should submit to the same thing myself. It needs to be official and without my knowledge." The XO nodded "And no one else should know. I haven't been able to track anyone else so as far as I'm concerned the only two people not double agents on this ship are in this room."

"I'll do it; I'll find this mole and burn them out if I have to. I'll be careful though." The Captain nodded.

"I think we should look to the crew officers first, they have the most access to the classified documents and would be far more likely." The captain turned to his desk and pulled out his document pad. "So focus on them first. But we also have received our orders from headquarters. This time they're sending us to an out of the way planet on the fringes of Galactic Company space. He brought up the report and handed it over to the XO, who connected it to his and pulled out the pertinent information.

"I'll work on plotting us a course. This should be easier than the last one though, that's for sure."

"Agreed." Said the captain.

Dan Reich

He liked this place, he had decided. It was a dark and sleazy place, but it had a nice charm to it. "Who am I kidding." He thought to himself "I belong here." It was bathed in the glow of a brown dwarf, like a dim light bulb about to go out. As a result, the dying system was like a large subterranean system spread out. The civilization was advanced, but the years of resource gathering had left it dependent on the sun for energy, and with the dimming of their star, so too came their culture. Vast high-rises now were empty, not having enough power to operate the advanced robotics to keep them up. The robots they did have were extremely efficient as a consequence, and he was after that prized technology, far more advanced than their own home world. They performed every duty here, cleaning, manufacturing, cooking, law enforcement, you name it. He chuckled to himself as he lit a cigarette, its end growing cherry red in the dark sunlight. It's a wonder the damn things didn't run the place!

He walked along the dimly lit street and down the slums that had been constructed after the great turning, the time the residents called when the star burned down from an orange to brown. That had been the kicker, what had turned off most of their technology. And that's when the Galactic Company came in and began buying up real estate and companies like they were hot cakes. It had not taken long before they owned half the planet and had a firm enough control on the government to absorb it into the Company. Now, after a few wars and a couple expansions and losses, the star system had managed to end up on the borders of the Companies territory, one of the last strongholds left on the outer fringes.

He had managed to get ahold of a couple less advanced robots and dissect them, stealing their technology and sending back up to the mother ship. They had become incredibly cautious after the last incident and now it felt like they were on their own, with almost no contact with the ship in the average month. Dan had been here for a few months now, and he felt like he was rushing against the clock. Tomorrow was his monthly contact day, the mother ship had been forced to hide on one of the moons and was only able to open up contact about that often, and he still had only been able to take a few energy harvesting and robotic technologies, all only minor improvements in what they had already. So that was what had led him to today's outing.

In the short amount of time he had been able to establish a few contacts in the robotics black market. He had gotten a few of his cache from them but he thirsted for the more advanced, newer models. He had heard stories about the AI system in them; it was light years ahead of the old, junky models he had been messing with. So he was meeting with one of his contacts to purchase a stolen model of the new military grade robot. Dan knew that these ones usually came with a locator device so he had not been surprised when the contact asked him to meet him for a rendezvous and enter an electronic damping warehouse.

He met his contact at the shoe store, hanging outside and buying a drink from the vending machine just as they had agreed. A shorter man walked up to him, features indistinguishable in the pale sunlight.

"And how do you find your beverage my friend?" the man asked. Dan had ordered the planet's special, a mixed, sweet drink served cold.

"Hot and spicy." Dan replied, confirming the code agreed upon. The man turned and Dan joined him in his steps, walking next to him.

"The warehouse is just down the street." He said "You can call me the Dwarf, and I will call you the Buyer." Dan nodded, tracking their progress in his head and with his internal map system. They were moving farther into the slums, and deeper into territory the local law enforcement rarely patrolled. It was owned by the underworld and the two held a shaky truce. The law only sent in robots, not its customary robot – human pair used everywhere else, and many of those never walked back out. But the ones who did return had generally caused a large enough body count to cause the underworld activity to pause, for a short time at least. It was the only way they could get them to stop, short of an invasion. And the criminals had no qualms about hiding behind innocent civilians so the law knew that that sort of action would have a high rate of innocent death.

They rounded the corner, and Dan spied the monstrous behemoth of a warehouse down the street. It was larger than all the other houses in the area and towered over them. The dwarf lead them down the street at a casual saunter, bringing them closer and closer to the dark giant. He didn't say anything else, and the silenced was natural, not strained. Dan had never been in this situation before, but he had dealt with some criminals. It wasn't the same as his brief stint as guard in the brig, but he did have the money and would be able to meet any demands they asked. He still felt a nervous foreboding, and he realized his jaw was clenched with nerves, a small ball forming in his stomach. As they got closer he relaxed his jaw, breathing and loosening up the knot in his belly. He concentrated on the breathing, linking it to his conscious and using his training to calm his body. Dan felt assured at the small weight of his concealed weapon, an old fashioned piece he found in a pawn shop one day when he was searching for his first models. And then they were there.

The Dwarf stopped at a pair of opening doors, opening one up halfway and stepping into the darkness. Taking a breath Dan steeled himself and stepped inside. The instant he crossed the threshold he could feel all of his electronic connections turn off. He powered down all his transmitting devices, but left his recorders up and running. Just in case, he set up an emergency beacon that would send out as soon as he was outside unless he shut it off. You never could be too careful, he thought. But he pushed the nagging thought out of his brain that if he needed the beacon, that would mean he was dead. The breathing exercises, he thought, focusing himself. He took a few seconds to look around at his surroundings. They had entered through the bay doors for loading and unloading, the deck free of clutter and devices. Deeper into the warehouse were stacked boxes, and various unidentifiable pieces of equipment. In all likelihood most of the stuff in here would be legitimate, a front for the criminal activity. A catwalk ran the length of the place, and straddled the rows and rows of boxes from the top. He could make out figures walking along them, probably the hired toughs for protection. They carried mean looking silhouettes, and Dan could only assume what they were used for. He concentrated back to the task at hand and followed the Dwarf.

The squat fellow had made his way and was heading for what appeared to be a half open box that had been resealed. As he got closer he recognized the figure of a model 3000 series defense bot, put into production by Robontic Industries, a local leader in robotics. Part of its chest had been removed, and various circuitry parts had been pulled out and now laid strewn about the table the box laid upon. A technician of some sort was hard at work, reassembling the demolished robot. Sparks flew from the tools he was using, but as they got closer, he noticed their approach and shut off the device.

"Ah, I was jus' finishin' up 'ere." He said, with a quite noticeable dialect. "I 'ad to remove the main tracking' device and a few o' the backups, but she'll be untraceable now, I guarantee." The man clearly was from the southern part of the planet, a place where a much harsher language had been developed. The dwarf climbed up onto a short little ladder clearly placed for the purpose and surveyed the handiwork. After a few moments he nodded to himself, and the technician seemed to relax a small amount. Whoever this man was, he clearly held some power within the system.

"Mister Customer, you want to have a look?" the dwarf asked, turning toward him. Dan stepped up to the box, looking inside. He pulled out an old fashioned magnifying glass and began to study the circuitry. The technician was fairly skilled, he had managed not to destroy some secondary circuits and energy harvesting devices, and had avoided the biomimetic muscles entirely. That was the real prize of this model, the material they were using was almost thirty times stronger than human muscle, and extended to a large range of temperatures, perfect for work that normal humans wouldn't be able to do.

"The tracking device?" Dan asked, looking up at the technician. He grinned and pointed to a small bundle of circuitry and wires sitting beside his tool. Dan picked up the mess and located the main transmitter and the three small backups. Everything was in order, this one should be clean. "If you can finish sewing him I would most certainly be appreciable." He put the mess back onto the table and turned back to the Dwarf.

"I expect everything is to your liking?" The small man asked pointedly.

"Yes, absolutely." Dan replied. He reached into his pocket, and slowly pulled out the transfer device. "I have the price we agreed upon, plus a small tip." The dwarf whipped out a reader and inserted the small card, running a program to determine the amount. He nodded when he saw the amount. "I may be in the market for follow-up business, not all quite as complex as this." Dan said, motioning to the robot. Whether it was true or not, and he did have some notions about some other pilfered robots, he didn't want to walk away from the table with nothing else to offer. People like that usually ended up with the short end of the straw, and by short he meant dead. The dwarf nodded, putting the chip away.

"And how would you like your merchandise?" He asked. The technician had gone back to work, putting back in devices and welding them back into place. Dan looked down at the unwieldy thing, thinking about his options. He didn't trust the dealer to actually deliver it, he had his money now so he had to walk out with the merchandise. He spied a hover lift in the corner and pointed to it.

About half an hour later Dan was walking out with his brand new contraband military robot. It felt good, and he let out a sigh of relief as he passed the door and felt his communications kick back in. just to be safe he had placed a scrambler on the robot, disrupting any transmissions it could have sent out. He had the hover lift in tow and made his way back to his apartment, avoiding the looks some were giving him. He avoided the major routes, but had to tap into his map system to avoid some commonly patrolled areas. When he had made it back to his side of town, robot hovering a few inches behind him, he fiddled with the lock to his lab and opened up the large doors leading inside, watching them sliding slowly and silently to the sides. He pulled the lift inside, and turned away once they had been safely and slowly back in place. He activated the lock and began to get to work.

He wheeled the lift into position and mechanically lifted the robot out of the box and onto the dissection table. He strapped himself into the driver's seat of his disassembly console and began to go to work.

"Let's see what this baby has to offer." He said to himself as he strapped on the control visor. He lowered the cutting device and began to disassemble the robot, piece by piece. His full body scans had revealed nothing, the robot's exoskeleton not only shielded it from radiation it also shielded it from his scans. Once all of the heavy alloy was removed though, he was able to have a better look. He whistled in surprise, amazed at the hunk of electronics. This stuff was far more advanced than the old model house robots he had taken apart in the past few months, this was a goldmine. He detected at least fourteen new energy harvesting devices that he had no idea how they worked, and the biomimetic technology was incredibly advanced. If he did not know it he would have thought by the look they had been able to copy a human almost exactly and upgrade the strength parts. But as he probed deeper he realized the true strength of this technology was its ability to interact. The AI system was the most advanced he had seen of its kind. A network of photonic wires ran through the entire system and connected it completely, like a huge web of the neural connections and nerves that run through the human body. With the photonic signal, and not an electrical one, the processor was able to run at speeds that far surpassed the electronic equivalents. In essence, the computer could think twice as fast as the human could.

Dan sat back in his chair, astounded at the tech he was able to gather. He checked his calendar, only a few more days until the synchronization. He could learn a little bit more, but most of this technology was far more advanced than he could understand. It would probably take years for the engineers back on the home world to reverse engineer this stuff, let alone the time it would take to put it into mass production and use. He lit the equivalent of a cigarette, a foul-smelling synthetic substitute and far weaker, and inhaled the smoke, feeling himself calm down. He held it in, he had adjusted to the stuff, and finally let it out in a long, slow stream. He would be busy in the next few days, he knew, but he took a small moment to relax.

"Sometimes it's the small things" he said aloud, to himself. Then he got back to work.

Stan Super

He liked and loathed this place at the same time. The weather, the light, most of the planet was just too depressing for him, but at the same time it hid him and enveloped him like a security blanket. I guess all spies like the darkness at some level," he thought to himself. He shivered in the cool air, and pulled his coat closer around his arms. He was looking out the city from the hospital balcony, on break from a surgery. He often wondered how all these targets had seemed to develop their own advanced medical system. But the more perplexing this is how it surpassed the home planets in nearly every case. From the holistic approach on the Green planet to the advanced triage and battle dressings of the abandoned world to the advanced cybernetics here in the Blank System, which surpassed their own implants. That had been the most surprising, out of all of them. Compared to the technology here it was like they had outdated computers in their brains. And they had taken the very best of the home world technology. The only area they had surpassed them was in stealth, while the Blank planet had developed in complexity, their implants and their functions were almost undetectable to any system in place in the universe. "We have always been crafty." He thought to himself.

"Doctor Super?" he heard a name call out. He turned, looking in the doorframe at the young and voluptuous nurse calling his name. She was quite beautiful, and he had developed somewhat of a crush on.

"Oh, Nurse Sally, please excuse me. I was just out here musing to myself." He strode back into the room and closed the door behind him, latching it securely into place. He picked up the chart of the patient on his mobile reader and browsed it, checking the symptoms for any advanced signs of rejection of the cybernetic implants. He had arrived at the planet with a cover story that had soon landed him at one of the most prestigious hospitals on the planet, albeit as a lowly paid general practice doctor. "I'll need you to have them run a few more tests, I've added them to the list already but I'd appreciated it if you checked up on them, I know you pull more weight with the lab techs around here." He was grateful for the chance to be working with Nurse Sally, but it proved to be a bit awkward at times, when she got too close, when her hand brushed his accidentally transferring files. He knew that any sort of relationship was doomed from the start here and he didn't want to bring himself to hurt her. That and whenever he felt himself get too close or his tongue start to say something to her his heart sped up and his tongue tied in to knots. He turned to see her standing by the patient's bed, gazing down concernedly at his sleeping figure. The look on her face and the pale sunlight coming through the large window made her look so beautiful. And the outfit complimented her well, although they were not designed for it. It only hinted at what was underneath, but from what he could tell she was very good looking there as well. He felt himself blushing at the image in his head and he turned, hiding his embarrassment and hoping she would not see. "Thank you Nurse Sally, I'll finish my rounds and head out for the night. Have a good night." He strode quickly from the door.

"Goodnight Doctor Super." He heard her say softly. He made his way quickly and furiously to his office, and stepping inside, leaned his head against the wall breathing hard. He did not know what was coming over him, here he was on mission and he was distracted by a school boy crush!

"Get ahold of yourself Stan!" he scolded, making a fist and pounding against the wall. The slight pain in his hand helped and he began to focus on his breathing exercises, bringing his conscious and subconscious together in order to control the wild emotion inside him. He felt himself calming and he allowed himself to relax, slumping down in the chair reserved for visitors. He realized how uncomfortable it was, but he slowly came back to himself. Nurse Sally may be a beautiful, charming, and well-endowed but he had no business thinking about her. He had to concentrate on the task at hand, he could not be thinking about her lips and how luscious they looked, tempting him to kiss"—he realized he had been thinking about here and angrily jumped to his feet. A small smile played across his lips as he thought about the ridiculousness of it all and he grabbed his mobile reader, which he had placed on the small table next to the entrance of his office and shuffled out the door, eager to do something to get his mind off her.

His first stop was an advanced limb replacement case; he dealt mostly with accidents and limb replacement, a man who had lost both legs in a manufacturing accident. He was the floor engineer, and wealthy enough to afford some of the better technology so they had sent him to his hospital, the Advanced Cybernetics Facility. They had been able to craft him two completely new robotic legs, complete with his own skin. They had upgraded the muscles so now he would be able to run longer and faster without feeling the effects and the support were rated to withstand higher pressures than before. Stan had analyzed the legs before he had put them in and they were truly an incredible piece of technology. They were also incredibly expensive, almost twice as much as his very nice apartment complex, which, although small, was still upscale. They had the same advanced materials on the home world, but the way these things were put together was quite incredible. The engineers back home were sure to have a field day reverse engineering everything he was sending back. From artificial limbs to ocular implants that detected every wavelength of electromagnetic wave to artificial organs with more efficiency to a small device that produced a slight constant stream of endorphins, he had seen the gamut working in the general surgery department. It was perfect for him since he was able to help the specialists with their projects, and he took a smaller paycheck than the specialists which the general manager liked about him. He was flying under the radar as much as he could, and that was just the way he liked it.

He continued on his rounds, visiting a few more patients, before clocking in and heading over to the hospital library. The literature on this planet was quite fascinating, and he did like a few of them. Some genres were incredibly morbid, one in particular was divided into how many of the opening characters remained alive at the end, the most popular being none. It provided some fascinating insight into the culture, which he found invaluable on several occasions, which helped him blend into the local populace. Dealing with people, he needed the in on how to put them at ease, and many of his tricks came from popular culture and contemporary dealings, which were better understood in the context of history. He selected one of the latest bestsellers and headed out the door, eager to be on his way. Tonight was his check in day with the mother ship and he did not want to miss the opportunity, the hospital had recently began using the most complex and complicated cybernetics in the last month, with the release of the new year's models, and he had information stored up that was itching to burn a hole in his pocket it was so hot. He got into his super high efficiency transport and set out for his rendezvous point, putting the thing on autopilot and settling down in the seat and opening up the book.

He arrived much earlier than he anticipated; the transporter had managed to slip just past the rush hour home, and got out to stretch his legs. Stan had discovered this place a few days ago, a small rise in the road that showed the spread of the city, and had loved it immediately. The brown dwarf was a small sphere in the sky, just beginning to sink towards the horizon, that gave off almost as much light as a full moon circling the home world. It cast long, dark shadows from the skeletons of the ancient high rises, the tops of which were inhabited by only the most extremely wealthy, who were able to pay to keep the elevators and life support systems on those floors running, and they shone like tiny beacons of wealth in the day and night, irradiating their owners power. Stan knew for a fact that the Center's Head lived in the shortest high rise; he made sure almost everyone he met knew that, but he really had no desire to go there. They were said to have luxurious parties often, where only the richest of the rich mingled. He pulled out a blanket and spread it out, taking his novel and a book light to read in the deepening shadow. He opened up his channels and waited for the mother ship to establish contact.

The darkness did get depressing after a while, and one of the biggest problems the Blank's had was with suicide. It was among the top killers, and did not have a cure in sight. This world was dying; the great lighthouses of the old culture the last vestibules of life left. They gave the sun a few more centuries at most, and for now it seemed like a giant angel of death floating in the sky. When it died it would take everything with it. It was no wonder that the most popular stories always ended with everyone dying. As he sat there, no longer reading, watching the sun slip down over the horizon; he could feel the last ragged breaths of the world being taken. He found his mind wandering back to his patients, then Nurse Sally, and all the acquaintances he had made during his months here. He felt a pang of guilt, most of the patients would be able to escape on the great life rafts that would most certainly come to their money's aid, but what about the less fortunate? In all likelihood, if they lived to witness it, they would not survive it.

It's here

Thankfully, the chances of the current inhabitants making it that far were slim to none; it was likely none would live the couple of centuries they gave the old star. That was, if they were not wiped out before then. The Blank system was part of a coalition with a long list of enemies. They had been forcing the coalition back for centuries, once this planet was near the heart of the Blank control, but now it resided on the outskirts of their territory. It was perfect for their mission, pre-occupied with so many other enemies they most likely would not be searching for Empire technology. But then, after what had happened with the last mission, they had taken great care to cover their tracks. Hence, why it took a month just to open up a channel. He checked his internal clock, and calculated the rotation of the pieces of rock quickly in his head. It shouldn't be long now. He pushed the thoughts of death and war and pain and sadness to the back of his mind and double checked his packages, making sure everything was there for the mother ship. Stan wondered how long they had left here, and quickly abandoned the thought as Sally entered his mind. He would not be ruled by his emotions, not again today at least. He felt a connection open up to the mother ship and immediately sent off his packages. He needed to stay connected while they checked the information, but he rose and got back into his transporter, starting it up. He was anxious to be done with it, the longer they were in contact was that much longer anyone else had to stumble in upon their transmission, masked as it was. He received confirmation that the information had been transferred successfully and requested information about the mission. The operator at the other end put him on hold, right now the rest of the infiltration team was likely checking in as well and the Captain and XO were sure to be in the room when it was. He sat, idling in the metal box. A few minutes went by, and he began to breathe again, concentrating his focus and dispelling the anxiety gripping him. It was taking too long.

He heard the other end of the line crackle as the operator got back on. He was advised to continue gathering information, it was unlikely they were going to be gone within the year. He sat back in his chair, slowly letting out a breath he had not realized he was holding. Over a year, and their deployment time was already far over as is. He made the customary checks and terminated the connection, slowly coming to grips with the weight of the words. It was true, most often his superiors overestimated in giving time estimates, in favor of it being shorter rather than longer, but the Captain generally tried to get as close to the actual time as he could. In all reality, that was probably around what headquarters had given him. He pushed the transporter into motion, manually taking control. It helped him think, and mull things over in his head. The roads out here were curvy and winding, never really straight until they got closer into the heart of the city. He descended from the small overlook, the ghettos and slums of the new city falling behind the facades of the actual ones. It was a shame to see those huge tenements go to waste, but reality was reality. This planet was nearly stripped of its natural resources, and had resorted to cannibalizing itself long ago. It was a wonder the things still stood, with how much material had been put into them, but it made sense that the government had left them standing, it did serve as a reminder to everyone, of the old and lost ways that had not worked out as well as they planned. He drove through the winding roads, mind stewing over everything in it. He knew exactly where he was going, but he dreaded going there. At the same time, he felt the anticipation run through him.

Stan arrived at the little coffee shop a long while later. The overlook was as far out from the inner city you could get, and on the opposite side of this part of town. The traffic had not been too bad, but bad enough to make him not look forward to the ride home. He stepped out of the transport, into the thin chilly air of the night, and locked it up, eyes wandering around the street. The dim light of the night lamps lit the semi crowded street for them and the machines moving by road. Most would be running on autopilot this late at night, the sensors allowed them to run lightless and save energy, but every once and a while the path was lit up by the cool blue light of a transport. He walked to the door of the shop and stepped inside.

Warmth met him as he passed through the airlock. It was not unusual for him to see one, but shops generally tended not to have them. When he opened the inner doors though, he could see why they did. It was cozily warm, unusual also, and filled with the rich aromas of a multitude of different brews. Stan breathed it all in deep, savoring the flavors in his nose. The bean did not grow on the planet, there was not enough natural light to grow it any bigger than stunted, and this particular shop imported it from a nearby sector. It was one of the more upscale houses, which they tended to be due to the scarcity of the product, but it was not the most fancy. He had met the owners a few months ago and he knew they were as cheap and frugal as Jan was which was saying quite a bit. He made his way to the counter, and was met by a bright eyed youth.

"Mr. Super, it's good to see you again, the unusual?" the young girl asked, Nancy was her name. He scanned the list of drinks, interested in something different.

"No thank you Nancy, I think I'm in the mood for something else. How's the coffee explosion?" she wrinkled her nose a slight bit, making a face.

"I don't think you would like that one, it's too strong. Maybe the Columbian blend? It's more mild and smooth than anything else we have." He located it on the menu and read the description.

"Sure, that sounds good." He handed her his payment chip and she punched in the order, the machinery whirring to life and buzzing as it worked on everything. Within a few moments it had processed the order and Nancy held a cup down to its nozzle, the brown liquid flowing from it.

"One Columbian Blend made to order." She said, smiling as she handed the steaming cup to him.

"Thanks Nancy." He replied

"You are welcome, Mr. Super." He took a small lump of sugar from the receptacle and added it to the cup, stirring it and taking his first sips as he moved away from the bar to find a comfy chair in the corner. He sat down and placed his coffee on the small end table in front of the chair and reached into his pocket to pull out the novel. He began to read, and a few minutes later, right in the middle of a riveting passage about a horrible transport crash that killed all the characters but the main one, he felt a tap on his shoulder. He looked up at the disturbance and his breath caught in his throat.

"I didn't know you were a literary critic Dr. Super or a coffee connoisseur" There, standing above him, Nurse Sally looked gestured to the coffee shop around her. She looked nothing like she did in her work uniform, her golden hair cascading down her shoulders free of any restrictions.

"Ah, Nurse Sally, I guess I could say the same for you." He replied as he noticed the cup in her left hand. He nervously cleared his throat in the awkward silence that ensued. "Would you please join me?" he asked finally, after what seemed like ten minutes. He stood up as she made her way to the chair across from him. She was beautiful, in an outfit that had recently become popular, and it was a tight fitting layer of advanced synthetic material that insulated against the cold. As she sat down, he also noted that it left little to the imagination, and although he was right, she did have an exquisite form, he began to feel his cheeks warm.

"How often do you come here doctor?" she asked.

"Please, feel free to call me Stan. I prefer it, especially outside of work."

"All right...Stan." she said his name with a hint of hesitation, and he could see a hint of red adorning her cheeks as well. He paused, confused at the sight. He did not quite understand these beings, the female side of the human species.

"Well, actually I have been coming here for quite some time now." He continued. "I've actually had something of a weakness for coffee and was delighted to find this place on an exploration excursion." He left out the details of the original excursion, a scouting expedition to find an alternate transmission point than his rented room. "What about you…may I call you Sally?" this time it was his turn to blush. His heart had started pounding in his ears and he could feel the silliness inside him.

"Yes, that's fine. Well, I'm not much of a coffee drinker myself, I much prefer tea." She said, raising her glass and pointing to the shape, it was a teacup and different from his own coffee cup. "But I have been here a few times, they occasionally have concerts here." He had heard, and he definitely had been careful to avoid them, crowd usually gathered in places like that and many people meant many things could go on.

"Concerts?" he asked inquisitively, leaning forward and taking another sip of his coffee. He put his book away, back into his special jacket pocket. "I know there isn't one tonight, and they usually are few and far between in this area, is that your only draw?" she locked gazes with him then, and he could see deep into her soul it seemed, but he could not tell what was there. It was like taking a drink from a cool, refreshing river, looking into those eyes, and they drew him deep into the brilliant blue of them. She finally broke eye contact and looked away, he had never realized how beautiful she really was, and yet she seemed so vulnerable. Her gaze had lowered to her cup, and she swirled it idly.

"Doc-" she began, but stopped. Flustered she continued on. "Stan, I-" she stopped again, and drew a deep breath. Calmed she continued once more, "you seem so distant" her eyes locked onto his again. "It's like you have a great weight on your shoulders that no one could ever bear. It hurts me to see you like that, would you tell me what's wrong?" he beautiful eyes stared into him then, hunting for the truth. But he could not provide it, he could not tell her how much it pained him to see this dying planet and work to steal its secrets while at the same time prolonging its life by a little piece by piece. It was worse enough that he was here as an enemy, but as an enemy in sheep's clothing he could barely stand.

"I-I can't save them all." He said after a short pause. It did bother him that he lost patients even with the advanced technology they had and the routine surgeries they did, complications still arose with the cutting edge machinery they were putting into people. He did the best thing that he could do, that he could think of, he told as much truth as he could dare. "I look around and see the death and it pains me." He hung his head, feeling the weight of the confession lift off his shoulders like a bad dream. Her hand felt his, and he looked up, with a slightly confused look on his face, feeling the same in his mind.

"I see the goodness in you Stan, and it makes me glad." As if she was just realizing what she was doing, she snatched her hand away from his. Things seemed to make more sense, but he could not really tell, what did she feel for him? "I-I'm sorry." Flustered she stood up. "I shouldn't have come here, I'm sorry." She turned and fled out the door, leaving her tea unfinished. He stood up to follow her, and realized that if he did her fate would be entwined with his. He watched her run from him then, and forced himself to sit back down. For a long time he watched her cup, watching it get cold unmoving.

Sam Harrod

Sam sat idly in his chair, watching the time creep by as he waited. It was really too bad that all bureaucracy's were this way, incredibly inefficient. As more and more people shared the power, less and less work got done. The greatest empires of all time were created on the backs of only a few people, usually a single empire. The greatest of all led by one man, whether it was the Mongol Horde or the armies of Alexander the Great things worked when one guy was in charge. He reflected on all the misgivings and failings of the same empires as well, but having a crazy leader was a small price to pay for the security, right? Sighing, he abandoned the play of words in his head and thought of something he could be doing. He had already hacked into the main systems and stolen quite of information from the government, but the real power laid with the enormous corporations and companies that made up the Blank. They had originally economically taken over the planet, and that was the way the kept things running. The real power houses on this planet were not the governors or rulers; they were the tycoons who kept the steady stream of cash flowing in and out of the systems. They were the ones who held the reins, and their systems were much harder to access. That was why he was here, trying to get access. The government post he had managed to secure had been a nice little taste of what he wanted, but he was trying to land a spot in a higher level company, as a consultant to the company head. He had no way to completely be sure his goods were safe, but he hoped the doctored documents would avert suspicion. Things were not quite as secure here as on Barkbeat, but it could have been a lot easier. They had conducted the interview already, which he had brilliantly blown out of the water, and now he was just waiting to see if he got the job. And wait he did, they certainly were taking their time.

He smiled to the receptionist as she walked by, documents in hand for some unknown purpose. He needed the access this job would bring, he just was not sure about what sort of access that would be. He was staring at the door when it opened, two men dressed in business attire exiting it together.

"Mr. Harrod, please come in." a voice called from inside. Sam stood up and casually sauntered in, nodding to the two men, they had been present for his interview but silent, who in turn returned the show of respect and continued on to whatever they were going to do. When he entered the office for the second time he felt more at ease, the beautiful wooden desk now no longer as imposing underneath the dim light coming in the window he was accustomed to. "Please, have a seat." The man said, gesturing towards the chair located directly across from him at the desk. The man was the Personnel officer of the company, and because he was applying for such a high level position, was conducting the hiring's personally. A carved wooden nameplate on his desk read "Malcom Xavier". Sam sat where he was directed, suppressing the nervousness and sinking slowly into the comfortable chair. Malcom pulled out a document, what Sam presumed to be his credentials, and scanned them once more. The man was older, balding and with a paunch that suggested wealth, and his face was adorned with reading glasses, and anachronism in the time when your eyesight could be fixed with a quick and painless operation. But here they were, on the bridge of his nose. The man looked over them at him now, and then removed them, placing them gently into a holding case.

"Well, I must say your credentials are outstanding Mr. Harrod." He began. Sam nodded in polite receipt, the standard on this planet and the man continued. "But I am afraid your skill set, although valuable, is not what we are looking for at this time." Shocked, Sam heard the words continue. "Perhaps sometime in the future we may have an opening that you might be able to fill, but for now I don't see you working for us. Thank you for your application and your time, Jenny will be able to direct you to where you need to go." In a daze Sam rose with the man, taking his outstretched hand. He thought for sure they would hire him, if his credentials stood up under scrutinization. Perhaps they had found him out?" he thought to himself. The danger of being caught brought everything back into focus, and he realized he had remained silent. Quickly he tried to recover.

"Thank you very much for the chance for application Mr. Xavier." He found himself saying. "I was humbled that you would take the time to even accept it, and was grateful for your interview. Please, if you do have an opening, let me know, and if it feels right I will not hesitate to accept. Good afternoon." Sam turned and found jenny, the receptionist, waiting at the door.

"Please follow me Mr. Harrod." She said, and let him out the door. At their desk she pulled out a small basket filled with expensive looking treats. A consolation prize. "We value your time and high standing, and we would like you to accept this gift on our behalf for applying." She handed it to him then, and he took them. "The elevator is down the hall and to your left." Unceremoniously she sat back down at her desk and began clicking away furiously; returning to whatever it was he had interrupted.

"Thank you." He said and turned, walking in the direction she had suggested. He could not sense anything different about her demeanor, or that of his interviewer to suggest that they knew. He supposed that if they had security would be waiting downstairs for them. He began to enter the elevator, then thought differently and decided to take the stairs. It would not matter either way, they would likely have secured a perimeter around the exits, but he thought it would cool his head and allow him to think. That had been his first and most solid lead, an opening mentioned in passing by one of his coworkers. If he was not caught, if he managed to get away, he had a few more less substantial job postings that had opened up. Each step his brain worked, each knocking of his foot on the metal staircase echoed in his mind, formulating a new plan. The sound spread through the stairwell and came back to him, echoing in the silence of the place. Although the elevators ran on schedules to save on energy, it was frequent enough for most people to take them. Like on the home world people still preferred convenience. He descended slowly, but soon was at the bottom, too soon. He forced himself to follow the breathing exercises they taught in training and slowed his pulse, calming down. Sam opened the door and pushed into the brighter lobby. It was sparsely filled with workers on errands or leaving early, but a quick scan of the place revealed no more security than at the front desk. He moved past them, and they let him go unhindered. So, if they had revealed him it would be to the police outside. It made sense, not allowing them inside the company property, so Sam continued to the door. He pushed the glass door open, tasting the cold air outside and letting it envelop him. There was no sign of lawmen. Breathing a quick sigh of relief, Sam turned and made his way home, carrying the package under one arm. Now either one of two things had happened; they were not suspicious of him and everything they tried checked out, or they had discovered him and were waiting for some reason. Although he was sure of his modification, he was not positive they were airtight, hell, he had thought getting the job was a sure thing. That had shaken his beliefs in himself quite a bit.

He did not go straight home that evening; he had to clear his mind. As he was walking along in the cool night along the crowded streets of the shopping district he realized that, for the first time in his life, he had been rejected. The academy had accepted him almost instantly, with his intelligence, and the service followed suit with their recommendations, and he was given almost totally leeway in the occupation most were ordered to. He wanted a bit of adventure, a way to travel around and see new things, so he had signed up for the infiltration service. Only in training did he realize how hard it was to be accepted into the program, which only took the best and brightest of the willing. Even on missions he had met with success, obtaining jobs and posts that most would not have even dared for, but he had always been careful and weighed the risks and rewards. He was not a gambling man, he was a man that stepped into things with great care and thought. But now, on this out of the way planet in a dwindling power he had been rejected, failing to do what he wanted. He moved through the crowds mindlessly, and as it struck him. He barked out a laugh, head held up at the sky, startling people around him. How ironic, they had probably rejected him for all the right reasons and probably did not even know it. He let his frustration out in his laughter, and soon was doubled up, crying in the street with laughter. People paused to stare at him oddly, a fully grown man in a giggling fit standing before them. It all came out then, his frustration and anger, his fear and loneliness, his happiness and joy, and he let it wash over him, the laughter cleansing him like the rain had on Barkbeat. His laugher eventually subsided and the pain in his stomach had gone away. He stood up straight, wiping the tears away from the corner of his eyes and chuckling. People still stared at him, but eventually they moved on, and he did not care. 'Well, he thought to himself "I guess that man knew what he was doing" still chucking every so often, he made his way home.

The next day at work, his daily quota already complete and his paper work already done for the day, he made his rounds, picking the brains of his coworkers and looking for any additional leads. It was common culture for people to start in government until they had secured a job and move on, especially in his department, the department of records. He heard a few new snippets, a job opening here, and position filled there, but was generally disappointed. Not only was it common culture, most of the workers were bad enough that the managers wanted them gone, so they too circulated as much information about openings as they could. He had one more interview today, something he had set up after his failure last night. If they did find him out, for some reason they were not using that information, or they were using it some way he had no way of knowing about. Returning to his desk after his rounds, he logged into the system and, after setting up the proper precautions, began to work his way around the systems, looking for some way into the company he had applied to yesterday, Quantro Products. Again, he hit the same fire walls and brick walls he had experienced every time. He sat back, studying the walls, looking for something else. Maybe he was doing something wrong; maybe he was coming at it from the wrong angle. He had already tried bashing into it, poking a hole in it, breaking through it, but all his attempts had met with more and more failure.

He quickly set something up, acting on instinct. He turned on his music collection, selecting a local song known for its interesting melodies and innovative ideas. He cracked his knuckles. This time, he was going to break in. he created a virus, packing it to open up a door through all the walls. He disguised it, putting layers of safety nets and deletion protocols on it in case someone began messing with it. And then he began to package it, putting it within a few images, layering it in and weaving the two strings of information together like a complicated fabric. When he was done he admired his handiwork, all created on a government system. Logging into the device connection, which linked almost everything together into one large space, he disguised his actions and searched for a connection to Jenny, the receptionist for his interviewer. It took him a few hours, but he managed to track down her information and soon discovered the golden prize he was looking for. It seems she had signed up with an online matchmaking service, and had been speaking with a few men in the process. She had browsed the information of a few men recently and he selected one, and disguised a message to appear as if it had originated from him. He choose one she did not seem too interested in, but had been looking at off and on.

"Now, let's see if this will work." He said under his breath to himself. He sent off the message and waited. Other people began to go home, saying their goodbyes in the office. Sam got up to stretch and grab a cup of local tea from the break room, terribly weak stuff, and spent a few moments chatting, all the while eagerly anticipating his message. When he got back to his desk she still had not opened the message, so he waited. Soon he was among the dwindling few in the office and he grudgingly shutting down his system.

That night at home he had trouble concentrating on anything. He was conducting a few experiments with the local bacteria, one particular strain was interesting. It had the ability to withstand extreme temperature ranges, from extremely hot to very cold, an unusual trait in bacteria, but would only eat certain sea plants with a precariously narrow potassium-nitrogen concentration. He had narrowed the concentration they like and was experimenting on if they would break down other substances with the same compositions, but he did not seem able to concentrate on it. Every few minutes online research he got the urge to stand up and walk around, breaking his connection. It did not help that in a few days he was due to contact the mother ship.

Eventually he gave up on the experiment and just began wandering around town again. He liked the open air markets they had, somewhat bustling but really quite dull. It seemed like it could be a good place to get a knife in between your ribs, but he was careful to scan the area for any possible followers that may be looking for a quick and easy target to rob. A few stalls were clearly fronts for some sort of unsavory business, burly "salesmen" accompanied by shifty eye shop owners, with little merchandise to sell, but he was in a rougher part of the city and expected that. Every once and a while he would stop at a half-empty stall and browse their wares, but mostly he just walked, and thought. Plans ran through his head, formulating ideas and conjuring situations. They all danced around, every once and a while two would touch and a spark would go off, but he would quickly dismiss it. Sam did realize that he may be in over his head on the Quantro Products business, if they knew what was going on he was sure they were not going to hesitate to move on him. In all likelihood, assuming they knew his credentials were almost all made up, they were simply observing him, not knowing his intentions. It would be obvious if he could just dig around their system for a few minutes, he was sure that most of the talk had been kept off the paper, but even the unsavory aspects of running a successful business needed some documentation, especially considering the types of companies that were successful in the Blank Quadrant. It all came back to the money, of which his paper trail was suspiciously clean.

They had been on the planet for a few months now, I guess it had been half a year" Sam thought, looking back to the day they arrived. They were smuggled on board a freighter they had found picking up cargo on a nearby asteroid mining project in the quadrant. The ore had been destined for Blank so they just waited for it to land and then quietly slipped off the merchant, split up, and started the mission, almost all completely from scratch. Sam familiarized himself quickly enough with the online system and had created some quick and dirty back stories, which he had gone back and solidified after a few more experiments with the system, enough to get them jobs and enough money to eat and sleep in a safe place. From there he had been able to set up a neat little fund that was financed by the Empire, enough to make them able to do what they needed to. He bought a yellow, a local fruit that resembled a pear somewhat from the home world and made his way back home, eating it along the way. The walk calmed his mind down enough for him to sleep, so Sam slept.

The next morning he went into work and quickly finished his daily allotment. The paperwork was not too strenuous, but he developed a couple of programs to do it for him, and pulled up his real work. He had just loaded his protections when he heard a small ding that made him smile. She had fallen for the bait. He watched the return message, slightly amused that she was also interested in "him", while he set up the anonymity protocols, enabling him to access the company records without giving away any information about himself. Once everything was in place and he was completely protected and silent, he slipped through the small hole the virus he had created had made in various security walls and began his hunt for the truth.

A few hours later his smile had vanished. He had managed to track down a few messages between Malcom Xavier and one of his superiors and was not happy. They had somehow seen through his credentials and were completely baffled by his case. Thankfully, the Empire did not have much of a presence in the area and the traffic suggested nothing of the truth, but they thought he was a spy for a rival company, which could be almost worse. They were waiting on a few more checks with some sister companies, but as soon as they found anything substantial they were going to move in on him and do something. Most likely, they would torture him for information then kill him. He could either spill everything or tell them nothing, either one would end with him dead in all likelihood. He needed to get off the planet now. He got up and clocked out of work, casually trying to chat with a few coworkers before he left, but soon he was out the door.

Back at his rented place he wiped all traces of his contacts with the other agents and quickly began to delete anything compromising he would be leaving behind. He had managed some headway into the advanced security systems, they would be useful back on the home world, and had everything ready to be shipped up to the mother ship, but he had two more days until they would be range for contact. For now he had some time, but he was not sure of where to go. He sat on the edge of his bed; everything he needed packed into a single bag lying on the floor next to the door. He was not sure of where to go, but he was sure he needed to get out. He looked around the room one last time, then got up and left, grabbing the bag on his way out the door.

He walked the first night, knowing that they would begin to follow his trail as soon as they realized he had fled. Two days, he had two days to think of some way to get off the planet so he could present his plan to the mother ship. Walking helped clear his mind, and the cool evening air helped even more. He headed the only place he could think of, towards the slums. People who went in tended to never come out again, and it did not matter if they were alive or dead. He hiked up his bag and walked away from the brighter lit places of his middle class neighborhood. Besides, they would think if he was running he would run away from the city, perhaps catching the nearest shuttle. They would never think he would be hiding right under their noses. Along the way he began to formulate a plan.

Sam had managed to find an out of the way room for rent, on a day to day basis, and had managed to stay out of trouble long enough to get there. It was a sad little establishment, clearly meant for the prostitutes who worked the streets to turn their tricks in, but the owner was used to the anonymity he wanted. He asked no questions when Sam presented him the hard currency, hard to find and hard to trace, that he had assembled for just such an emergency. The owner had only squinted at it, pointed down the hall and gave him a key. The room held a dilapidated bed and a small lamp, with a rickety window overlooking the street below. He had expected no more, but with his equipment he would be able to access everything he needed and he found a power outlet in the corner, of which he fashioned a makeshift charger to plug into. "At least I have that." He thought to himself.

The dim light of the sun stretched into the almost non-existent light of night, but Sam just laid on the creaky old bed still. He was not thinking of a way to get off the planet, he was not thinking of the mission, he was thinking of his family. He was an only child; his parents had been in a province that only allowed one child per family, but his parents had done their best to make sure he was never alone. He was surrounded by other children and animals, cats and dogs usually, but he always ended up being by himself. He missed them, it had been four years now, even longer since he saw them last. He remembered that day; it was when he graduated basic training. They had been so proud, he remembered, a small smile coming to his lips. His mom had hugged him so fiercely, and he thought he saw tears in his father's eyes as he told them he was going away. Sam felt sadness come over him, and he curled up in his bed. He could barely remember what they looked like. He drifted off into sleep, his mind troubled but his body exhausted from the day's journeys.

He awoke the next morning, the dim sunlight filtering through the dirty windowpane. He bolted upright, his surroundings unfamiliar.

Then everything came back to him, and he jumped out of the bed, realizing he had overslept. He changed his clothes, exchanging them for a new pair and hooked up all his equipment to his nexus. He had an escape to plan and only today and tomorrow to plan it.

He nodded to the owner as he left, who did not even give him a passing glance, and stepped out into the barren street. As far as the slums were concerned, he had picked a mediocre area, neither too rough nor too neat. He had a few items to locate, and he had a hunch he knew where to find them. He turned down the street, to the market he had passed through on his way here last night. A few inquiries into a stall appearing to be selling nothing earned him an audience, and he was shown into a back room where the real business was carried out. A grizzled old man opened up a secret door in the room, which appeared to be storage shed, and showed him into the shop. It was littered with contraband, mostly weapons, and a few hard to get items that seemed legitimate. Sam quickly found a few items he was looking for and haggled over the price, paying far too much for them. A few more excursions into the underground and he had assembled what he needed, but more importantly, he had a name. Most of the items were not that bulky, and he was able to make it back to his room without attracting too much attention, something you did not want in this place. He dropped everything onto the floor and checked his cash supplies. Sam groaned. "This had better work" he said to himself "I don't have enough money for a second chance." Tapping into his funds was out of the question now, not showing up for work would earn a little bit of concern and a chewing out the next day if it was only one day, but two days was sure to set off the alarms and sent the government into a search, although they would not search too hard considering his low ranking. Still, a search would set off alarms in the Quarto system and spark a possible search there.

The rest of the day he spent assembly and constructing with the help of his network and calculations. He went to bed with only a rough starting point, and spent half the night tossing and turning, unable to sleep because of the horrible feeling in the pit of his stomach. He awoke early then he planned and used the time, building and preparing. His meals were cold, taken from his provisions, and that's all he stopped for. He finished around mid-day and found himself sitting alone in his room, plan ready and instruments assembled, everything ready to go except the permission he needed from the higher ups. He secured everything as best as he could, locked his room and went out to search for a good spot to open a channel to the mother ship. He found an abandoned high rise with access to the roof and made his way up there. The place was filled with squatters, mostly women and children, of which he ignored. He sat in a corner on the roof, back against an empty water receptacle. A few minutes later he felt the ping of the mother ship and opened up a channel. Birds flew lazily in the sky as he conversed quietly. Soon he had finished and Sam stood up. He took one last look over the city as evening began to descend and he returned to his room.

Back aboard the ship an exhausted Sam stumbled through the mess on his way to the sickbay. Crew members crowded around him, eager to see him and hear his stories.

"What was it like Sam?" Asked the Navigator, Sebastian Branch.

"It was incredible, like riding an angry bull, only the bull is on fire and could explode at any moment. It was exciting." He was exhausted, adrenaline nearly gone. The Doctor pulled him out of their grasp, shooing them away like flies. He poured some hot soup into his mouth, along with a few pills and walked him out the door.

"He'll have plenty of time to tell you what happened after he has some rest, leave him alone now." The crew members watched them go grudgingly, a few members staying behind to talk about it.

"What happened" the weapons officer, John Smith, asked.

"You haven't heard yet?" Branch said, pulling up a chair as the crew crowded around him. "He was compromised, apparently got in a spot of trouble with a few local business men. Anyway, so he was compromised and had to get off the rock real quick, so he bought up a bunch of parts, strapped 'em together into some crazy contraption and rode the next ship out of there." A glint in his eye told the crew there was something else.

"Go on!" Smith pleaded, eager to hear it.

"Well...the first ship out of the spaceport was a Company Cruiser." They all stared at him in awe.

"You mean to tell me, he snuck onto a Company cruiser before it launched, and then got out as soon as it got into space?" Smith asked doubtfully.

"Snuck onto one, no." Branch paused for effect, looking around his audience. "He rode it, clamped to the outside, and shoved off at an angle. We picked him up halfway to the moon."

The Sixth Planet

The Captain peered over the document pad at his agent, studying them. Stan Super had been his crewmember for five years now and could not believe what he was hearing.

"You want to go back?" he asked incredulously.

"Yes sir. I-I developed feelings for...someone." He blushed; the Captain could not believe it, Stan blushing like a schoolboy! Well, after everything they had been through so far he could hardly be surprised. He dropped the document pad onto his desk and rubbed his eyes. Turning to look out the porthole into space. It was beautiful, but every day was a challenge, his crew kept reminding him of that. He turned back to Stan, who had gone silent and expectant.

"You know I can't do that Stan." Stan visibly slumped at the words, but he nodded.

"I didn't think so- it was worth a try." He said, his face showing acceptance.

"Stan, I don't know how much longer this deployment is going to last and everyone's itching to be back at home with their loved ones, but I can't make an exception. Not only that, you're talking about a possible breach in protocol. We warn our agents about attachment before they go down for a reason. The only way you two would ever be allowed to be together was if she was naturalized or you became a fugitive. You're too valuable to the Empire."

"I know, I know...I knew all of that going in. I-I, well, I just don't know what to do. What should I do captain?" Stan looked at him expectantly, hoping for some sort of answer he could cling to. "What can I do?" The Captain paused, remembering his own weakness, and he reached up to feel the locket around his neck.

"You do what everyone else does Stan, you wait. You do your duty and job, but you remember her, and you always keep her with you. And you hope, you hope that she remembers you too." He could feel the weight of remembrance in his hand, and it weighed him down. They sat in silence, two men brooding in their own thoughts.

"You're right sir." He stood up to go, then paused. "I think the hardest part was saying goodbye, and knowing I might not ever see her again. I asked her to wait for me Captain, am I selfish? Knowing that I might never come back, and promising her I would, was that wrong?"

"It will only be wrong if you don't keep your promise Stan." The captain said. With that, he dismissed him and Stan left his office. The Captain turned to stare out the porthole, lost in his thoughts.

They received their new orders in the middle of drills. The DCO, Peter long, received the coded transmission and alerted the Captain, who was in engineering surveying the drills. He reported to the bridge and cut short the drills, asking for the message to be sent to his office. He passed crewmembers on the way, seeing the expectation in their faces. He really wanted this to be good news. He sat down and paused, taking a moment.

After he read the message he called in the XO. Not surprisingly, he was only a few moments in coming. The word of the message had probably spread like wildfire through the ship. The XO took the chair and waited, face grim, knowing the Captains moods and realizing it was not filled with good news.

"How long this time?" he asked. The Captain paused, collecting his thoughts.

"How long has it been Joe?"

"Four years and eleven months, two days sir." The XO responded.

"It seems like it was just yesterday I was staring out a shuttle window, gazing on what would be my ship. Do you remember the day we took command?" the XO nodded, his features smoothing as the Captain took him back in time. "I said we'd get back Joe, and I mean to keep my promise. It's going to be a little bit harder this time. We have orders to Tempest."

"The water planet?" the XO asked.

"That would be the one. The main objective is their underwater technology, for obvious reasons. The new recruits are taking longer than they expected, they're giving us two more years."

"Two years!" the XO exclaimed, bolting upright in his seat. The Captain handed him the message, and he took it, staring at the screen. "I'll get the crew to work on it right away."

"Have we cleared anymore?" the Captain asked. This topic may have been the harder one to talk about. The XO shifted uncomfortably in his seat.

"The infiltration team is clean, as far as my investigations are concerned, and you as well." They had agreed to look into them first, they were less likely to be the double agent, since they had less access to the ship's records, but they had to be sure.

"My work came to the same conclusion the Captain said "and my initial sweep of the records show no signs of the identity, let alone anything that could possibly give us a lead. Whoever this is has access to the transmissions, is very good, and has not made a mistake yet."

"It's an officer." The XO stated. The Captain paused, then nodded. It made the most sense, although they were already better compensated then the enlisted crewmembers. It smelled of one of them, but he could not put a finger on which one.

"Agreed. Fortunately and unfortunately we have an intelligent and competent set of officers. It won't be easy to find them. You focus on the investigation and I'll look into their records and past. Between us both I hope we can figure this one out." He left the rest unspoken, because if they could not figure out who was the mole it would likely destroy them all.

Jan Young

It was raining again, it was always raining here. It brought down her mood and made her unpleasant to be around. Jan stared out the window, scowling at the raindrops. She could not control those either, although the Tempest locals had somehow managed to control theirs. They liked it, a planet covered in 95% water and they wanted more, it baffled her.

"Miss Young?" One of her students had approached her desk, she had easily and readily slipped back into the role as teacher, and she turned to him.

"Johnny, what are you doing?" she snapped at him, more harshly than she intended. "You startled me" she said, calming down and re-assuringly patting his shoulder as he seemed about to cry. It was all this rain, it just got to her. "Are you having trouble with the problems?" she asked, more motherly this time.

"Yes Miss Young, I can't figure it out." He replied, looking less startled than he had. He pulled up his workbook and pointed to a half attempted problem.

"Is anyone else stuck on problem thirteen?" she asked. A few hands shot up, and some more followed timidly, all from the back of the classroom. She did not care what anyone thought, competition was a good thing and she still made them compete for head of the class, although the teaching system was completely different. The basics were still taught, language and mathematics and the like, but the rest of the curriculum was student based, where their strengths and weaknesses were determined by the computer and the lessons were tailored by the instructor. They were in the middle of group instruction, as the basics were called, and she stood to explain the problem.

"Thank you Johnny, you can take your seat now." She stood and he returned back to his chair. Using her whiteboard she explained the problem as simply as she could. "Now remember class, the first step you take in problem solving is to determine what your problem is, and what you need to do. If you look at this closely and read the problem more carefully you will recognize the improper fraction." She scribbled the question on the board. "You are given everything you need in the problem, you just have to relate it back to it, does that make more sense? A few of them still looked puzzled, but she did not continue explaining the problem. Sometimes experience was a far better teacher than she could be. "Don't give up, if you get stuck look at it from a different direction." The class returned to their assignment, and she returned to her work as well.

She was trying to access the weather controlling technology, for both personal and professional reasons. It was far more advanced than on the home world, essentially nonexistent, and would benefit crop development and other productions. That, and end this incessant rain. But she knew that she could not do that, steal technology and then use it on the same place? It was just a pipe dream, one she wished would happen, but she was not that careless. Instead, she started infiltrating the weather system, a complicated bureaucracy and network that was loaded with useless information and red tape. So far she had set up a fake access code, but was only able to view the unclassified documents. She had programs running, trying to break through their tight security measures, for some odd reason they had better security here than some of their military technologies, but so far it had proved unsuccessful. She checked them again. Still running to no effect.

By the time she looked up again, it was nearly time for the school day to be over. She stood up before the bell could chime its end, and before the students would cause a mad rush to be out the door.

"Now remember class, determination occurs this Friday so be prepared." Determination was the final testing before the seat order was determined; it was held to create a metric for progress. It tracked the progress in the basics of the children, a quick and dirty test compared to some she had seen carried out, but it made no false claims that it was unbiased or enormously worthwhile. It was just another tool she had as a teacher, and she could over rule its findings if she thought they were wrong. A bell chimed softly in the background, and the students began to quietly pack up their things under her watchful eye. When they had gone Jan sat back down and quickly viewed the results of the assignment, the programs they provided the teachers were extremely helpful in grading everything by themselves. She noted with satisfaction that most of the class had managed to obtain the right answer for the question Johnny had asked about. When she had finished her work she herself packed up and went home.

She preferred the underground corridors to the exposed walkways in her travels. They were well lit and clean, and there was no chance of getting wet. Jan traveled them now, walking the familiar white tunnels back to her apartment.

The authorities found her later, lying face down. She was cold by then, reported in by a passerby walking the unused corridors on a midnight jaunt. The upper levels were unusually precarious during the midnight storms, so he had been forced down to the underground level to avoid the mess.

The lawman scanned her body. She had been stabbed twenty times, but it looked like the first had been in the kidney, a perfect killing blow. The pain had silenced her before she died, and no one had heard a thing in the area. He suspected a professional, although her purse had been ransacked and her jewelry had been stolen, it did not feel like a normal criminal act. As they were taking her away, he looked into her eyes, open with surprise and pain.

"Who wanted you dead?" he murmured to no one in particular. The one obvious thing he could see in the case is that whoever it was, they certainly got their way.

Later that day, in the office, he was called into the head lawman's officer. When he left, he was even more puzzled. The world agents were taking over the investigation, an odd move for a common crime. Whatever had happened in that corridor was far above his pay grade. He quickly put the thought out of his mind, turning his attention to the paperwork piling up in his inbox.

Aboard the Ship

The first few missed check-ins they had assumed she had gone into hiding, but now they had found out the truth. Agent Yellow, Jan Young, was dead. She had been stabbed in an alley; they had salvaged the information from her still responsive recorders. It was no ordinary killing, whoever had done the job was a trained killer, and the Captain feared the worst. It seemed the double agent had claimed its first life, there was no other explanation. She had been on the surface over a year, deep undercover, and no evidence had pointed to anyone accessing her false records. It was if they had found her and eliminated her on the same day. The Captain held the document pad in his hand, brooding over the results of the investigation. The agent had accessed the transmitter and covered their tracks, but his search had been more thorough this time. It was hard to relay a message back to the home world and then on to the enemy, but that is exactly what this spy had done.

And now he had a firm profile in his head. With months to go on the deployment, the entire operation was in danger of being blown wide open, the cover of one of his agents already compromised with barely a thought. They had decided against pulling out the remaining agents, the information on each was immediately scrambled and stored inside the vault, accessible only by him. It may have been too late, but the agents had been warned and had gone into hiding. They needed to root out this mole, and careful contact had provided him with a plan, surprisingly devious, from Dan Reich. He hoped that this had worked, they had narrowed the options and only two officers seemed likely and remained as suspects. They both had access to the same information, higher than the normal crewmember, and they both were intelligent and good with the transmissions. The captain wished in his heart that it was all a mistake, that he had been wrong every step of the way, but he knew they were not. Somehow a mole had snuck in under the guise of a crewmember, and was working for the Galactic Conglomeration, trafficking information through a complicated series of steps. It had been far worse when they worked on the Barkbeat planet delving into their information, but the Conglomeration was eyeing some of the territories in the Galactic Company systems and was currently in friendly talks with the Company. It would be in their best interest to share information, especially about the Empire's espionage movements.

He had assumed they knew about all four agents, but were not able to locate the other three. Jan had given her location to the home world in a standard report they found a few days later, at least a general one, and it would be easy to set up a tail if the mole had provided images of her. The others had been lucky, at this point they had not revealed where they were located in and working around and had remained as anonymous as possible, even to the ship. He wished he had warned them about giving away too much information, but he knew the mole would have gone into hiding the instant they would have smelled anyone on their track, and he needed to flush them out. Now he was determined to save the rest of the operation and take out the mole in one fell swoop.

The Captain stood up, stretching his legs and pushing away the finished dinner. Standing by his porthole, he had eaten in solitude tonight; he admired the awesomeness of space. They were close enough to a gas nebula to view it unassisted, and it shimmered and glowed with the light from the system's star. He hoped and wished that this worked; he could never live with himself if he lost another person.

Dan Reich

He liked the rain here, like he had liked the darkness on Blank. It made him feel more secure, knowing that his actions were obscured by something. He slipped through the cold and rain, working his way to the tower. He nearly lost his footing, slipping on the smooth metal, but he regained it before he could fall. He checked his safety cable one more time, cursing the robotics on this planet.

"You think they could develop a hunk of metal that could go fix this thing." He muttered, inching his way along the roof until he reached the tower. He grabbed the metal rungs, clinging to the relative safety of it as he looked down from where he was. The planet was made up of mostly water, but the colonists who settled here had built their own land effectively. There were floating cities and cities underwater, but the larges were built above the waves or on the small amounts of land that remained. The great bubbles of the buildings rose up, some into cylindrical skyscrapers tipped with weather controlling spires. That was where he was now, perched perilously on a tall tower, shorter than some, but high enough to make his stomach flutter when he looked over the edge. The buildings were made up of a coral like material harvested from farms beneath the waves, they grew like flexible trees underwater in many different varieties and the colonists had taken to calling them water trees, they had discovered early on that they made great building materials. Not only were they impervious to the water and did not break down in it, most forms were clear in nature, and tough and flexible.

Unfortunately, they were also extremely slippery when wet, a fact he knew too well from experience. He did not know what he was signing up for when he got this job, but he learned quickly he did not like heights as much as he thought he did. It was one thing flying high in the air in a ship or airplane, and quite another to be dangling out in space attached to a building by a thin cord. It helped a little that the tether was strong enough to support the dropped weight of a tank, but not by much. He frowned and looked up at the long spire, and then began to climb, detaching his cable from the roof supports and attaching it to a track that would move up with him, but slow his fall and stop him gently if he did. And then he began to climb up through the pouring rain, one rung at a time. Dan decided not to look down, focusing on the shortening distance up.

The weather spires were deceptively tall, and took an hour just to climb to the top. When he finally arrived at the junction box, the guts of the device, he took a nice little break, sitting down on the platform constructed for maintenance, feet dangling out in the rain hundreds of feet in the air. His tether firmly attached to the tower, he could tell from his grip, he caught his breath. A small let up in the rain began to occur as it came down less hard, and the clouds quickly dissolved above the city, an effect of the weather spires. From his vantage point he could see the whole city lay out below him, and it was quite a breath taking sight. The construction workers were like artists, merging and splicing spherical buildings onto every available plot of land. Much of the new construction now was being added to the towers themselves, small bubbles seemingly growing out of the sides halfway up or at the base, wherever the owners wanted. After a few minutes of rest, he got back to his feet and back to work.

The constant cycling of the weather spire had done its damage, causing a collapse of some of the mechanical pieces he was still trying to figure out. He had gotten most of it down in the few months they had been on the ball of water, but he was still trying to work out the more sophisticated intricacies of the system. The spires generated fields of electromagnetic waves to affect the high nitrogen content in the water, much higher than that of the home world. Using the fields they were able to collect or disband the clouds, and change the amount of water molecules in them. In this way they were able to make it rain harder or softer, or even stop or start the weather if the storm was not too powerful, but they were still trying to figure out a way to slow down the occasional enormous storms that came through and ripped up the working pieces of the spires and damaged the houses. Lightning was the hardest problem to deal with, the spires themselves tended to create a lot of it with all the energy they ended up dissipating into the air, and lightning strikes had helped break some of the pieces, it happened routinely. He slowly but surely began to take the broken pieces out, putting them into an empty bag he had climbed up with attached to his hip. He had another one, filled with his tools and replacement parts, and carefully began to replace them. The sunlight slowly disappeared as he saw the clouds moving back over the city, electricity crackling from the working weather spires. He wiped the sweat from his brow, taking a break from his work. Without the clouds the heat from the sun became almost unbearable, rising far above the hot 100's, sometimes reaching 150 degrees Fahrenheit. The extreme heat of the sun, due to its closer proximity than that of the home world, contributed to the rainy nature of the planet, it evaporated the seas when the clouds dissipated. The cloud cover itself blocked most of the rays, cooling the planet, but the rain itself was always warm from the heat of the clouds itself.

The rain came down in a slight drizzle at first, and Dan hurried to finish his work. He had been up on the tower for hours now, and night was coming soon. He took the opportunity to scan the new parts, an upgrade from the broken technology as a replacement, storing the information for transmission back to the mother ship. The mission had been eclipsed by the recent developments, but he kept to it, trying to salvage as much as he could if the mission were doomed while not arousing any suspicion. He had tidbits and occasionally bigger information, but nothing that would give the engineers back on the home world a breakthrough. Right now his priorities were elsewhere though.

Finishing the repairs, now in the pouring rain, he steadily packed up everything for the descent. He had learned the various levels of rain since the long months he had been stationed here passed by. There was the lighter morning rain, the pattering lunchtime rain, drizzles, monsoons, hurricanes, and floods. But it continued, they had mists, wet fogs, patches, soakings, cloudbursts, and torrents, easily the most famous. At least, those were the only ones he had been in personally. Dan looked up one day that there were over three hundred classifica-tions of rain, and not only included the amount, but the compositions of water and types of clouds they came from. It was a big, watery mess. He started the descent, easily the hardest part of the job, and made his way down one dripping rung after another, his tether safely attached to the restraining hook traveling alongside him. It took longer to climb down, and soon the light through the clouds began to grow more and more dim. He tried to move a slight bit faster, careful to not look down now that he was suspended in space and not sitting on a platform, and soon he had made it to the roof, with enough time to get back inside before the last bit of glow faded from the sky, obscured by the rain and clouds. The rain had let up a little since its pour at the beginning, but he was readily soaked to the bone. He headed home, the water dripping off of him, through the various covered walkways. They did not keep all of the rain, but they did block some of it. Trying to block it all would have resulted in a leaky roof anyways, but the drain systems generally took care of the standing water, everything sloped down to them in one way or another. The paths themselves were almost pyramidal, coming to a crown in the middle, and it felt like he was walking on the side of a mountain constantly, but that was for the really hard rains.

He got home safely, which was a wonder between the walkways designed for their roughness but still seemed to remain slippery and the threats looming over his head, deep within the mother ship. He had thought about it himself once. Turning coat tails and switching sides. He really did not see the gain in it though, what employer would trust you when you had already shown them that you would switch sides for the right price or reasons. Plus, it was too underhanded, not honorable. Dan believed that there could be such thing as an honorable spy. He stripped off his sodden clothing, throwing them into the drying bin by the door, and took a shower. They had plenty of water for that, and he liked to get the grimy rain water shower off his body with a nice clean one. It helped a little, and he warmed up some food to eat. He logged into the local network as he ate, taking his mind off of everything by watching the local news. They had the standard tree dimensions, but the resolution just was not the same as the home world. Part of it was the water; most of it was the technology.

After he finished he shut the production down and checked the time. Now would be good enough he supposed. He opened up a connection to the mother ship.

"Mockingbird this is Agent Green." Dan transmitted, turning his thoughts into a message. That was the hardest part of training, in his opinion, trying to shut off the rest of your brain so they did not receive a blast of information and images. He had to wait a few seconds and retransmit; the weather here was not good for interplanetary communication. He tuned the transmission, increasing the wavelength to get better piercing through the clouds and tried again. "Mockingbird this is Agent Green checking in."

"Go ahead Green." He heard in response a few seconds later.

"I'm going to need a little bit of assistance down here." He started. "Some of my electronics are going haywire; I think the weather spires are interfering with them. They just upgraded equipment and it's been happening ever since they put the first one in." some of it was true; they were putting in new equipment at least.

"Standby, I'll alert the higher-ups." He waited as the line went blank. He was masking his transmission, and doing all the normal protocol established to not tip off the mole. He held everything out of his mind, not wanting to give anything away. Instead, he concentrated on his breathing exercises, calming himself down. A few minutes later it flared back up again.

"Green, this is Branch. Do you have any more specifics about the problem?" Branch was the Navigator, a good guy, and smart to boot. Dan was glad he had been the one on call today. The thought of him being the mole changed it a little bit, but he was still a likable character.

"Yes, well the local area, the cistern quadrant, has been a little bit more distemperate than usual. The underwater colonies were not affected but the surface city has experienced a lot of breaking equipment. The old spires weren't able to handle the increased load so they upgraded them." It was just enough information to locate his city, but he had to give the mole a little bit more. "I'm uploading a few scans I took of the new tech; I replaced a broken unit in one of the towers today. Everything works; it's just a bit sluggish." There, he had added the icing to the cake, and the trap was set.

"We have it now. We'll analyze this and get back to you sometime this week, it may be a little bit too complicated for us to handle so we may have to send it back to the home world." The customary ping receipt had sounded, confirming the upload.

"Roger, that's all I have to report today, I'm still working on the weather tech. Logging off now." Dan powered down after, cutting off the power to his equipment. It had all the basic elements of a trap, but none of the weaknesses. Dan sat back on his lounger. All he could do was wait and hope it worked.

Confrontation

He received the report within a few minutes of the end of the transmission. His document pad beeped, and onscreen he could read the details. The Captain allowed himself a small smile, the timing could not have been better, but the trap looked almost perfect to him. Dan had given away enough information to pinpoint his location without saying it straight out, and had even given away his occupation! It was almost certain that most cities only had a few maintenance men for their weather spires, and since they rarely broke down or needed maintenance he had blown his cover perfectly to the mole. He looked towards his door, as if he could see the whole ship laid out before it. Somewhere on this ship a double agent was working to bring this operation down, and he would find him very, very soon.

The door chimed as the Captain was staring at it, the sound startling him out of his trance.

"Come in." he called. In walked the XO, as serious as ever. He waited for the door to shut and took a seat across from the Captain before he spoke.

"Everything is set up and is ready to go." He said.

"And now we wait?" the captain asked.

"And now we wait." He agreed. The mole had thrown them off by routing their transmissions back to the home world once before, but this time they had all their ears trained on anything leaving the ship. Like they had grown accustomed to, they sat in silence, the weight of the unspoken words hanging above their heads.

It was late in the dead of night when a loud beep awoke the Captain. The Xo had taken the first watch, and they had rotated monitoring the ship on two hour long shifts, and it had been three shifts. He rolled over in his bead and sat up, the lights turning on at his command. He quickly began dressing while he opened up a channel to the XO.

"This is the Captain, what have you got Joe." He said, stepping into his uniform.

"We picked it up a few moments ago sir, it's going through a series of encryptions and is being bounced around the ships transmitters so I'm not sure where it's coming from." The xo replied, voice hushed as he was on the bridge in the Captain's chair, under control of the ship.

"Where's it heading? Or can you tell." The captain asked.

"It's definitely going back to the Home world. I'm tracing the origin now, Jesus Christ it's like a web! It's being transmitted from the home world connection, from at least fourteen possible locations. I'm sorting out the static now."

"I'm on my way up now." The captain said, slipping on his shirt and stepping through the opening doors. "Roger, I'll see you when you get up."

"Hurry, I don't think we have much time." He had made it to the bridge doors, his office and sleeping quarters located down the hall. The XO was frantically tapping on the control console, the rest of the bridge in sleepy midnight watch status, monitoring their stations. He cut the late night crew lately, down from its required force, he did not see the need for it, and so only the critical stations were manned. They had begun rotating positions early on, and by now almost all the crew was proficient at each, and all of the officers could man every single one, if need be. He walked up to his chair, the XO sliding out and letting him take control. "I started ruling out origination points, it was faster than trying to trace the damn thing. Whoever it is is good, really good. So far I've cut out the bridge, engineering, and your quarters." The main three places they could come out from, besides infiltration control.

"And infiltration central?" the captain asked. The XO still was tapping, and the Captain began to check the progress, looking into a few minor places here and there.

"I'm accessing that now...umm..." the XO kept tapping. "nothing." He said at last. The captain, working at random, tried sickbay. Somehow, the port there was not responding. His instinct flared up.

"I think I have something." He said, rising from his chair. "Check it, we need to know for sure." He paced over to the weapons locker as the XO worked. "Junior Officer Long, Crewman Davis and Crewmen Hutchins, front and center." The three members of the crew, who had perked up at seeing the captain in the middle of the night watch and were staring at the two, bolted to their feet and quickly made their way over to him. The Captain pulled out three blasters, set them to disable mode and handed one to each man. They looked down, confused. The remaining members of the watch, two Basic crewmen manning the ship status and steering, were wide awake now. That locker was never opened, not even for drills.

"You three will be coming with me, there's been a mole aboard this ship and I mean to catch it tonight." He secured a small pistol from the cabinet and then the Captain locked it back up, securing the remaining weapons.

"A mole sir?" Junior officer peter long asked, mouth open in shock and hanging.

"Sir, you can't go!" The XO protested, "I'll lead the team, it could be dangerous." The captain paused at the XO's outburst, and realized he wanted to do this, but it was not his place. He pulled the pistol out of his holster, handing to the XO.

"Be careful, I don't want you dead." The Captain said, clasping him on the back.

"I'll make it." He said, meeting his eye contact. Then, he turned and headed towards the door. "Alright men, I want Davis and Hutchins on the flanks, Long you're the rear guard." The door barely made a whisper as it opened, and the party exited the bridge to hike the short distance to the sick bay.

The captain returned to his chair, directing the remaining men back to their posts. He quickly pulled up video of the sick bay, projecting it on the main console. His face tightened when he saw the sight.

"Men, take a good hard look at the traitor who nearly sabotaged this mission." The Captain said, his voice as hard as steel. They glanced at the screen, but returned their focus to the man sitting in the Commander's chair. He had become something terrible to look upon, his face clouded and his posture upright. Neither man said a word; they only went back to what they were doing. "Joe, how close are you to being in position?" he said, opening a line to the XO. He had selected three men for good reason, the sickbay had two entrances.

"I left Long and Hutchins at the aft entrance and am making my way to the main bay doors now; I should be there within a minute." He heard back. Before the captain his programs had intercepted and decoded the transmission, and he saw every damming word. It gave updates on the ships position, the agent actions, and included a lengthy work on the location of Dan and his objectives, including recommendations for termination, all addressed to members of the Galactic Conglomeration. "I'm in position now." He heard the Xo say, in a soft whisper. The man on screen continued his work, trying to relay the message from the home world on to his contacts. His efforts would be in vain, now that he had been discovered. The captain opened a channel to the sickbay.

"Doctor Pratt." He said calmly. The man froze in his work, still over the interface. "You are hereby remanded to custody for the charges of treason and espionage. Give yourself up quietly." The law was particularly harsh on spies and he had the right to execute him aboard the ship, providing a proper investigation found him guilty. Being caught in the act was never a good sign though. The doctor had dropped his hands to his sides, unmoving in the dimmed light of the night lights.

"Well, I guess this is it then." Quickly he sprung to his personal console and began to access it.

"Take him!" the Captain bellowed, and then all hell broke loose. The two doors opened almost simultaneously, and a pistol appeared in the Doctor's hand firing wildly at the aft door. The crew returned fire, but he had dived behind a sick bed, and the energy harmlessly deflected off the metal frame. They moved quickly to get a better angle, and soon it was over as soon as it had started, the doctor writing in pain on the floor, weapons activated and aiming at the traitor.

"I'm coming down." The Captain said, giving control of the ship to the navigator, who had stumbled in.

Within minutes the Captain strode through the doors of the sick bay, jammed open from the firefight. He saw JO Long on one of the sick beds, his arm being tended to by one of the weapons specialists. Thankfully, it was not serious, after he checked on him, then continued to his original destination.

The doctor sat in one corner, hands and feet bound.

"He was trying to erase his records, but we managed to stop him." The XO said as the Captain squatted down to eye level with the man, looking deep into his eyes.

"I told this ship I would get them home, and that includes you. I just hope you like the cold, dark prison they throw you in." the doctor remained silent, and dropped his gazed to the ground. The Captain stood back up and turned to the XO. "XO, let's get those agents off that planet. And begin to plot a course for home." He looked around at the battle damaged sick bay. "We've been away from home far too long."

Epilogue

RETURNING HOME

"Empire this is Mockingbird 1274 requesting clearance to land." Officer Branch called away at his station. They were approaching the docking port and would soon be within range. The crew was at their battle stations, eager and ready, for the day had finally come.

"Mockingbird 1274 you have clearance to land, proceed downrange to the next waypoint." A voice buzzed in from the docking station.

"How long has it been Joe?" the Captain asked, turning to the XO. He grinned.

"Six years, three months, two weeks, and twenty five days Sir, and change." The Captain returned the smile, feeling giddiness inside him.

"Captain, we are within visual range." Branch called out.

"Put it up across the ship." The Captain ordered.

"Aye aye Captain." A few moments of tapping and Officer Branch relayed the image throughout the monitors of the ship. Gasps and sounds of awe rippled through the bridge crew as they gazed at the beautiful sight. The docking station was built into and through an asteroid the size of a small planet that had been trapped in the gravity well of a nearby white dwarf star and now was in stable orbit. The image was breathtaking, the asteroid glowing with the lights of the station set directly into the center of the great white star. The image had filtered all the extreme intensity of the star out and they could see its solar flares dancing huge distances from the surface of the great ball of gas. The Captain too felt himself caught up in its beauty, until the XO got ahold of himself.

"Don't forget your duties!" the XO barked, and the hush that had fallen over the bridge was broken as embarrassed crew members returned their eyes to their consoles. The ship moved steadily towards the small dot of an asteroid and it began to grow, getting larger and larger on the screen. It soon grew so large it eclipsed the white dwarf and the image adjusted to the new light, bringing out the intensity of the space port working lights.

"Empire this is Mockingbird 1274, we have reached the first way-point and are commencing turn one." The view began to change as the ship turned slowly to the right, and they began to make out the docks of the Empire.

"Mockingbird 1274 we have cleared you to land in Bay Seven, proceed to the coordinates uploaded now on the course." The voice responded. To many ears throughout the bridge it was the voice of an angel, leading them to a promised land. Two years away from home was normal for most crews, and even three was almost unheard of, but many things had gone wrong since they had left. The ship continued on its course, turning once more, then steadily moved to the open dock. A hush went over the bridge as they got closer and closer, everyone holding their breath in steady anticipation. The ship slowed and eased its way into the opening, restraints poised along both sides. She slowed down even more, slower and slower until it was just a creep. And then the Mockingbird stopped.

The restraints lowered onto the hull, bolting the ship and making it a part of the station.

"Mockingbird 1274, you are docked. All conditions green, welcome home." A cheer went up throughout the ship and bridge, the relief of six long years on mission finally completed. The crew was overjoyed, some hugging, some weeping, to hear those words they so desperately desired. The Captain smiled, clutching something in left hand. It was a locket, given to him by someone dear. He brought it up to his lips and kissed it.

"I've come back." He whispered.

Eclectic Stories

Thank you for spending your precious time reading this book.

If stories make you salivate, learn more about lore, take an exclusive sneak peek behind the scenes, and get writing updates in my newsletter, Eric's Eclectic Stories.

As a bonus you'll get *Stories from the Deep*, a Patmos Sea Fantasy Adventure anthology that gives a glimpses of lore, extra prologues and epilogues, and character backstories.

If you aren't satisfied, unsubscribe at any time.

Join at erickercher.com.

-Eric Kercher

Also By Eric Kercher

Patmos Sea Fantasy Adventure Series

Fathomless Pursuit

Architect's Prize

Ironbound Path

Sunken Prey

Unanswered Prophecy

Hardened Pilgrim

Final Peace

Seventh Hall Chronicles

Seventh Hall
Ode to the Survivors
Bastion of the Deep

Epic of Hornblood Castle

Siege of the Unfinished Keep
Winter at Hornblood
Branch of the Everlong

Castlebound Adventures

Rats in the Cellar!

Anthologies

Red Eagle Anthology
Searchlight Anthology

About Author

Eric Kercher was born and raised in a small town on the Great Plains on good books. After attending a small state school on the east coast he joined the US Navy to serve his country and explore the world. He worked on submarines, and the world beneath the waves captivated him with all its mysteries and wonders. After spending time in larger cities, he's settled down in a quiet town with his wife and children. When not on an adventure in a good book the author enjoys creating dust woodworking, architecture, and spending time with loved ones.

Find out more at www.erickercher.com.